Hound-dog Man

BY

FRED GIPSON

Harper & Brothers Publishers
NEW YORK

HOUND-DOG MAN

COPYRIGHT, 1947, 1949, BY FRED GIPSON

PRINTED IN THE UNITED STATES OF AMERICA BY
KINGSPORT PRESS, INC., KINGSPORT, TENNESSEE

Hound-dog Man

TO MY WIFE TOMMIE—

The real Blackie said of her: "She's too pretty to work. A little old girl like that, a man ought to put in a picture frame and set on his mantelboard, just to look at!"

Hound-dog Man

1

I WAS twelve that Christmas, too old for Santa Claus, but still too young to take a great disappointment with any grace.

All that fall, I'd saved my cotton-picking money to buy presents for my folks. I bought Papa a brass-studded dog collar and a lead chain. I got Mama an enameled cake-mixing pan that was just the size to feed a dog out of. And after spending that much money on them, I still didn't get the hound-dog pup I'd been pestering them for.

I felt like I just couldn't stand it, I wanted that pup so bad. All Christmas morning I sat around in front of the fireplace, feeling cheated and resentful. I thought some about running off from home, only I didn't have any place to go.

Finally, Mama called from the kitchen: "Cotton, have you washed and combed for dinner yet?" And I said, "No'm." And she said, "Well, you better be getting at it, young man!" So I got up and went out on the back gallery where the wash pan sat on an old sewing-machine stand.

The water was in a cedar bucket hanging by a chain from the rafter. I rattled the dipper in the bucket so Mama would hear me and I even poured a little water into the pan. But I didn't wash. It was a sunshiny day, but anybody knew that at Christmas time all water outside of a teakettle is too cold to wash in. I hadn't done anything to be dirty anyhow; so I just dipped the tip ends of my fingers in the water and wet down my hair a little, hoping my cowlick would save me a combing. It almost never did, but sometimes I got by.

I heard Papa come in the front door of the house

and holler at Mama. "Put on an extra plate, Cora," he said. "I see Blackie Scantling's coonhounds rounding the bend."

I began to feel better at that. In the kitchen I heard Mama say, "Oh, my!" in that voice she always used when Blackie Scantling came just in time for dinner. Mama didn't have much use for Blackie Scantling.

I gave my cowlick a quick pat and ran through the house to where Papa stood at the front door. I was glad when Blackie came, and I think Papa was, too. Blackie always had a lot of talk that was good to listen to. He was the best coon hunter in the country and owned the best coonhounds. He knew where all the foxes denned up and where the wild turkeys roosted and whose watermelons were getting ripe and where was the best place to catch a mess of catfish or shoot a bait of squirrels. Blackie knew all the things that I never got to learn, going to school like I did.

Some day I was going to grow up and own some crackerjack trail hounds and spend all my time prowling the woods like Blackie. Me and Spud Sessums. Me and Spud, we ran together a lot and we'd talked it over and made our plans. We might even go to live with Blackie in his old shack over on Birdsong Creek if Blackie wanted us.

I looked down the lane. Yonder came Rock and

Drum, all right. Rock was a long, lean red hound with droopy ears and the saddest eyes you ever saw. Drum was blue-and-white spotted, just as long and lean as Rock and just as droopy eared—almost as sad eyed. But they both carried themselves proud, padding along side by side each with tails keen as buggy whips waving high over their backs. Together, they lifted their heads and hit a faster trot. I guess they'd got wind of the kitchen.

Behind them a ways came Blackie, hobbling along in a pair of bad-fitting shoes. He was as long and lean and hungry looking as his hounds. He wore an old floppy hat and a brush-frazzled jumper. He packed a .22 rifle in his left hand and had a flour-sack bundle slung over his right shoulder.

I knew what was in that bundle; it was Blackie's party clothes. Blackie packed his party clothes along wherever he went; he never could tell when he'd run onto a dance or a candy pulling.

Blackie traveled sort of bent over, searching the ground for sign as he came. It sure had to be a cagy varmint that could hide its tracks from Blackie.

Rock and Drum came up and jumped the yard fence and headed around the house toward the kitchen door. Blackie stopped at the yard gate, fumbling in his jumper pocket with the same hand that

4

held his gun. He pulled out a fresh possum hide and waved it in the air.

"Looky what a big boar possum I got!" he shouted.

"He's sure a big un, all right," Papa said.

"Pulled him out of a holler stump back of Dub Sessums' corn patch!" Blackie said. "Son of a gun! Wouldn't sull a-tall. Went on the fight and had Rock here half et up before the old fool got over his surprise. He sure had his gall!"

I ran out to look at the hide of a possum with the gall to make fight at a coonhound. I held it in my hands and rubbed the soft fur against my cheek and got to feeling bad all over again, thinking: *Now if I had me a hunting dog, I could have caught this old fighting possum.*

Papa said: "Come on in, Blackie. The woman's got dinner ready."

"Dinner!" Blackie said, his sharp face showing surprise. "Is it that late a'ready?" He twisted his head and puckered his blue eyes to look at the sun. "Dogged if it ain't!" He looked down at the slits he'd cut in his shoes so his toes would have more breathing room. "Now, Brother Joe's woman Pearline," he said, "she's sure going to be put out with me. Promised her I'd be there by good sunup."

5

"You've missed it some," Papa said. "Come on in and eat your dinner."

Blackie took another squint at the sun. "I better git on," he said. "I'm rushed for time, Aaron. Brother Joe, he's got a scattering of frost-opened cotton, and I promised his Pearline I'd help her scrap the patch. She's bent on picking enough to make her a sleeping mattress."

Papa didn't say anything to that, and Blackie waited and looked uncomfortable and started fingering a snagged place in the knee of his pants. He looked up at Papa again, and still Papa didn't say anything. He just stood there pulling one horn of his black mustache and let Blackie squirm and fuss around some more at that hole in his pants.

I could see the devilment in Papa's black eyes and knew what he was up to. It hacked me. It wasn't right for Papa to plague a grown man and a friend like he did me sometimes, so I said: "Mama's done set you a plate, Blackie!"

Blackie looked relieved. "Well," he said to Papa, "I hate to put your woman to all that trouble, just to eat and run. But that's what I'll have to do—just eat and run. I promised Joe's Pearline I'd be in that cotton patch by sunup this morning."

He took the big possum hide from me and hung it

on a gate post and packed his gun and party clothes
inside the house. He put them down on the bed that
was spread with the new white counterpane Mama'd
got for Christmas. He laid his hat on top of them,
then stood and started running his fingers through his
hair.

I sure did wish I had hair like Blackie's. It was coal
black and shiny as a crow's wing. It was always sort
of shaggy around the ears and neck, but it curled up
to a mighty pretty ducktail in the back. I would have
swapped off my cowlick for that ducktail any day and
thrown in a good whittling knife to boot.

Mama came in from the kitchen, her face red from
the heat of the stove. She said "Dinner's ready," and
"Hello, Blackie," all in the same voice, and I saw
her company smile quit on her at the sight of
Blackie's things piled up in the middle of her new
counterpane. And when her eye lit on the pants
Blackie wore, she could just barely keep from frowning.

Blackie always showed the best kind of company
manners around Mama, but it never did help any.
Mama just took another look at those pants Blackie
wore and went on back into the kitchen.

Those pants had belonged to Papa up to a night
about a month back when Blackie's hounds ran

7

something up a hollow post oak on the yonder side of Bald Ridge. Blackie had climbed the tree and dropped some lighted matches down inside the hollow till he'd located the fox hiding in there. Then he'd pulled off his coat and pants and stuffed them down the hole to keep the fox in while he came to the house in his red drawers. He'd hollered me and Papa out of bed and borrowed the chopping ax. Me and Papa had got up to go see the fox race; only when we got there, we found the tree had caught fire and burned to the ground and, of course, burned up Blackie's fox and clothes, too. On a cold frosty night like that, it was only neighborly that Papa take Blackie back to the house and give him a pair of pants to wear home.

But Mama hadn't seen it that way. And when Blackie hadn't bothered to bring them back, she was sure put out with him. They were just old patched-up duckings and I guess Blackie thought a good borrowing neighbor like Papa wasn't going to be fussy about one pair of old worn-out pants as long as he had a couple of pairs without a hole in them.

And Papa hadn't been fussy. But Mama claimed she hadn't sat up half the night patching those pants for that trifling Blackie Scantling to frazzle-out in the brush.

8

Papa said: "You want to wash up and comb, Blackie?" And Blackie made a careful inspection of his hands and guessed it wouldn't hurt none to soap off some of the possum smell. So we all headed for the back gallery.

That's when we heard a dog yelp and Mama's voice lift sharply from the kitchen. "Get out of that bread, you wretch!" she scolded.

The dog yelped again and knocked over a can and went out the kitchen door, squalling like he was being killed.

Blackie ran out on the back gallery and said, "Confound that old Rock dog!" He grabbed up a claw hammer lying on the washstand. Old Rock rounded the corner of the house with his tail tucked, juggling a hot biscuit in his mouth, and Blackie threw the claw hammer at him, but missed him a good piece.

"Now, you stay out of that woman's bread, you old devil!" he hollered and then went into the kitchen and apologized to Mama.

"I declare, Cora," he complained, "I don't know what gits into them old hounds. At home, they won't set foot in the kitchen or touch ary thing they oughten. But go any place, and dog take it if it don't look like they just try to outdo theirselves!"

Mama put her stick of stove wood back in the box

9

and said, "That's all right, Blackie!" But she didn't say it the way she told the preacher it was all right the time a horse of his tore down half the front-yard fence. I noticed that.

She lifted a plate of hot biscuits off the stove, set them on the table, and stood back, waiting for us menfolks to sit down.

My face got hot, thinking how Mama had lit into old Rock with that stick of stove wood. What if she'd happened to've killed him or even broken a leg. I sure hoped Blackie's feelings weren't hurt about it.

We sat down to hot biscuits and fried chicken and nobody thought to look and see if I'd really washed or combed my hair. Blackie had got out of washing the possum off his hands, too. I guessed we could thank old Rock for that. Thinking about this, I felt a whole lot better.

I tucked my chin as Mama bowed her head to ask the blessing, but Mama was too slow. Blackie had already picked up his fork and stabbed a biscuit on the far side of the table. He bit into it and said to Papa: "You're sure in luck, Aaron, picking out a biscuit-cooking woman like Cora. These here biscuits is smooth and round topped as dry-land terrapins."

Papa laughed, and I saw some of the anger leave Mama's face. Mama was kind of proud of her biscuit-making.

"You take Brother Joe's Pearline," Blackie said. "Them little old biscuits she makes, they'll squat to raise and bake on the squat ever' time."

Mama even smiled at that.

Blackie reached and speared a pullybone and went to work on it.

Papa said, "I figured you'd have a cook back of your stove by now. Judging from the amount of varmint trails you've been picking up around old Ike French's lime kiln lately. I hear tell his girl Amy was combing the town for you last Saturday."

Blackie looked startled. "She was?" he said and shot an uneasy glance at Mama, then turned around and pitched a clean-picked pullybone through the window behind him.

"I guess that don't amount to nothing," he said. "You know how it is. No woman's going to put up with a yard full of old hound-dogs like I keep."

I saw the devilment in Papa's eyes again. "And between women and hound-dogs," Papa said, looking at Mama, "I guess you'd pick a hound every time."

Out in the yard, Rock and Drum started a fight over the pullybone. Blackie wheeled. "Dry up, out there!" he scolded.

"Well, plague take it, Aaron," he said to Papa, "you can't find a woman that'll put up with what a hound will. You take a dog like one of them yonder.

11

You can starve him half to death. You can run him till his feet's wore off to the bloody bones. You can git on a high lonesome drunk and kick him all over the place. But he's still your dog. Ready to lick your hand or warm your feet of a cold night. Now, show me a woman that'll do the same."

Papa rocked back his head and roared with laughing. Mama got up with a quick jerk and went back into the kitchen, wearing that tight look around her mouth again.

Blackie's eyes followed her. He looked uncomfortable. "Now, I've went and made her mad," he said. "Dog take it, I run off at the mouth too much."

I wouldn't say so to Mama, but I sure agreed with Blackie. Give me my choice of a good coonhound or a woman, and I knew for certain which I'd take. Couldn't any woman start a coon trail.

Mama came back and finished her dinner, but nobody said much after that. Papa kept grinning, though, and glancing at Mama, and it looked like Mama got madder at Papa than she did at Blackie. Finally, we all got up and headed for the fireplace room.

"Well, I sure hate to just eat and run," Blackie said, "but I got to git on."

"Better stay and let your dinner settle," Papa said.

"You wouldn't want to go right to work on a full stomach."

Blackie stood for a minute, poking his finger into that hole in his pants while he studied on that. He glanced at his stuff on the bed, then back to where a backlog of mesquite wood burned in the fireplace.

"Well," he said, " I guess a man ought to set and visit a spell after eating another man's grub. But I can't stay long. I promised Joe's Pearline I'd be there by sunup."

He wouldn't take the chair Papa set out for him. "Got plumb out of the habit of setting on a chair since Ma died," he said. He sat down on the floor, bracing his back against the wall. "Old chairs, they all got broke up and I takened to setting on the floor. Now, seems like I can't git no rest any other way."

I sat down on the other side of the fireplace and braced my back against the wall like Blackie. But pretty soon Mama made me go help her dry the dishes. When I came back thirty minutes later, Papa had left to go cut some wood and Blackie lay sprawled on the floor, snoring gently.

Mama was out in the kitchen rattling the pans for supper cooking when Blackie snorted a couple of times and woke up. He propped himself up on one elbow and looked around.

"I'm gittin' just like a big boar coon," he grunted. "Prowl all night and sleep all day!"

Papa put down his newspaper and got out of his chair to go kick up the fire. A shower of sparks popped out around him, and the chimney started roaring.

"Blackie," he said, "you recollect that old bob-tailed coon we treed on the Llano at Bee Bluff?"

Blackie sat up, his blue eyes awake and shining. "Lordy, yes!" he said. "Him and them hounds knocked Brother Joe down and fought all over him. I can see Brother Joe right now, down on his all-fours and that old coon perched up in the middle of his back and slapping dogs sky-west and crooked."

"And getting knocked down every time he tried to get up," Papa put in. And Blackie said: "Yeah, and them fool pups what can't git hold of the coon, gnawing away at Brother Joe's shanks and elbows!"

Papa rocked back in his chair and laughed and Blackie slapped his leg and added: "Lordy, but that was the maddest old boy from here to yonder! He'd a-kilt them pups in a minute if he could a-got up."

I'd heard about that coon fight before, but I never got a full bait of hunting talk. Something warm and shiny and sort of lonesome took hold of me.

"We sure raked in the coon hides that time," Papa said.

"I reckon!" Blackie said. "We wound up with plenty of money and six bits over from that trip." He shook his head and frowned. "But we had coonhounds in them days, Aaron. Why, that old Nigger dog of your'n, he could snuff the cobwebs out of a coon's track and tell you where the varmint aimed to prowl tomorrow night. Ain't no more coonhounds like that old Nigger dog!"

I sat on the floor by the fireplace and listened and watched through the window at the daylight fading and felt sad because all the sure-enough good coonhounds had played out. Then I thought how glad I'd be just to have coonhounds as good as Blackie's. It wasn't fair for Papa to have owned a coonhound like Nigger when he was a boy, and now him and Mama wouldn't let me keep a dog of any kind. I could feel a crying mad coming on, just thinking about it.

Blackie said, "Seems like boys don't git out and have the fun we-all used to."

"No," said Papa. "Nowadays, I reckon, their time's too taken up with books and school."

Blackie's face showed disgust. "Dog take it," he said, "looks to me like all that writing and reading's a waste of a youngun's time. Liable to ruin his shooting eye . . . I never worried myself with it. Ain't missed it none, nuther."

Blackie sure thought like I did. I wanted to jump

15

up and say, "That's what I been trying to tell you, Papa!" But I knew it wouldn't do any good. Sometimes of a night, after I'd been listening to Papa and Blackie talk hunting and fishing, I'd lie awake and cry a little. I was that eager to get out in the woods and have some of those big old romping times like boys did in their day. I knew I never would amount to anything, wasting my time on school nine months of the year and then hoeing cotton and corn all summer. But I'd done quit talking about it to anybody besides Spud Sessums. I couldn't make Mama and Papa hear to it.

Papa sat and stared into the fire. I could tell he was recollecting back. "You reckon," he said, "the coons is still that thick along that part of the river?"

"Dave Wilson says they are," Blackie said. "He's looking after that old Dillon Ranch down there now. I was talking to him in town last Saturday and he says there's a big acorn crop this year and the coon tracks is thick as fleas on a dog's back."

"I'd sure love to give 'em another round," Papa said.

"Well, what's holding you?" Blackie hollered. "Why don't we throw a quilt and a side of bacon into a wagon and go give 'em a round?"

I saw Papa's eyes light up, then he remembered and shook his head.

"I couldn't get off," he said.

"Why not?" Blackie wanted to know. "It's Christmas time and too wet for land breaking. There ain't a thing in the world to keep you here!"

Papa frowned and looked uneasy. "Well," he said. "I'm fixing to butcher a hog this week; Cora wants to get her sausage up while the weather holds good. And anyhow, Cora's scared to stay by herself of a night."

Blackie looked disgusted again; he reached back to pull at his ducktail. "Yeah, that's how it goes," he grumbled. "Let a man woman, and he ain't fit for nothing no more. He's tied hand and foot!"

Papa stared at the fire some more and didn't answer.

I was too excited to hold off any longer. "I could go!" I told them. I stood up, shivering all over. "It's Christmas time and there won't be no school till after New Year. We could take the mare and that old buckboard. And I could go tell Spud and he could go, too!" I couldn't stop talking, I was so excited.

"By gollies!" said Blackie, "we'll just do it. I been laying off to go ever since I talked to Dave Wilson."

Papa looked at me, startled. "You're a mighty short-tailed rooster to be talking about going off on a big hunt like that!"

"I'm as big as you were!" I said. "I'm twelve and

that's the same old you were the time you-all caught that bobtailed coon. I know; I've heard you tell it time and again!"

Blackie laughed. "By gollies, he's got you up a tree, Aaron. You wasn't as big as he is, nuther."

"But he ain't never been out more than a time or two," Papa said. "He don't know how to take care of himself."

" 'Course he don't," said Blackie. "And he won't never know till you let him out!"

"Well, I don't know—" Papa said.

"Dog take it, Aaron!" Blackie said. "The way you and Cora keep this towheaded youngun cooped up in the house, he won't be fit to knock in the head, time he's got his growth. You think a baby coon can set in his den and learn to catch a frog? Good lordy! He's got to git out and prowl the river banks."

I was wanting to go so bad, I could just barely keep from begging. But I knew how mad Papa got when you begged. And it was plain Blackie's arguing was packing more weight than mine ever would. I shut my mouth and waited.

"Well," said Papa finally. "It's going to take some old tall talking to convince your mama. But go tell Spud and then get up the mare and feed her. I reckon Blackie can look after you boys."

Papa was right. It sure took plenty of talking to convince Mama. She was still plaguing him about it after we all went to bed that night. I lay on my corn-shuck mattress in the shed room and listened to her. She wasn't talking out real loud, but she wasn't whispering, either.

"You want our boy to grow up to be nothing but a no-account fiddle-footed rake, Aaron Kinney?" she said. "With never a thought in his head but to run wild in the woods with a passel of pesky hound-dogs?"

"No, Cora," Papa said. "But a coon hunt now and then ain't going to ruin him. I was on a few myself and got over it."

"Yes," Mama pointed out, "but that was because I laid the law down about dogs. Hadn't been for that, you'd still be fooling away your time in the woods, same as always. And we wouldn't own a rag to cover our backs."

"I expect you're right about that, Cora."

" 'Course I'm right, and you know it," Mama said, starting in afresh. "I can't see why you'll let our boy leave home to go off with a bad influence like Blackie Scantling."

"Now, Cora," Papa argued. "Blackie's a pretty good sort of a duck."

"Good for what!" I heard Mama pounce. "What's

he ever done? Has he ever married and tried to make a home? Has he raised any children and done a lick of work to feed and educate them? What's a man good for if he dodges that kind of a duty?"

"Maybe he wasn't lucky like me," Papa said, teasing her. "Maybe he never did come across the right woman to steady and settle him down."

But Mama wasn't to be sweet-talked. "Right woman!" she scoffed. "In the last fifteen years, he's had chances a-plenty. And what's he done about it? Just left back of him a trail of heartbreak and regrets. It isn't marrying that Blackie Scantling's after!"

"No," agreed Papa, chuckling. "But Blackie's never kept it a secret what he *was* after. And I never knowed him to have to get rough with a woman, persuading her."

That made Mama madder than ever, and she lit into Papa all over again. But I wasn't worried now. Papa would hear her through; but if she couldn't put up an argument to convince him, Mama could talk from now on and not change his mind.

I did wish, though, that she would talk a little quieter. Blackie might hear her.

Blackie had bedded down with an old quilt on the floor in front of the fireplace. Papa'd tried to get him to sleep on a bed, but he wouldn't do it. He claimed his clothes were too dirty to sleep on Mama's white sheets. He said he'd got out of the habit of sleeping on a soft bed, anyhow; he'd laid out in the woods too many nights. He said he'd had an old bedstead his ma had left him when she died, but he'd finally broke it up and burned it for firewood, just to get it out from underfoot.

I hoped Blackie couldn't hear Mama giving him down the country, like I could. Blackie was sure a fine man. He saw things the way I did. Look how he'd stood up to Papa for me. Nobody but Blackie could have talked Papa into letting me go on a big coon hunt like this!

I lay quiet and listened to see if he was awake and hearing. But I guess he wasn't. His snoring was still regular when I went off to sleep.

2

IT WAS shivery cold at sunup the next morning, with a touch of white frost fuzzing the patch of rescue grass growing under the big live oak out in front of the house. Papa helped me and Blackie hook up the dun mare and load the wagon with our camping plunder.

"Now, you listen to what Blackie tells you," he

told me. "You get hurt or sick or something and your mama'll sure lead me a dog's life!"

Rock and Drum came out from where they'd slept under the doorstep and ran circles around the wagon, bawling and wringing their tails. They didn't have to be told we were going off on a coon hunt. I wondered if they could smell the good feeling inside me.

Blackie stood beside the wagon and poked his finger around in that hole in his pants. He said to Papa: "I guess Brother Joe's Pearline will think I'm a good un, going off like this when I promised to help her scrap that patch for mattress cotton. But dog take it, somebody's got to go along and take care of these little old younguns!"

Papa said to me, "Well, it looks like you're all set for going." Then he grinned and added: "When you get this wagon bed loaded with coon hides, you better come in."

"By gollies," Blackie declared, "if them coons was thick down yonder like they used to be and we had that old Nigger dog, we'd flatten them wagon springs to the axle."

Mama came out to the wagon with a sack of Christmas candy. "You'll want sweetening before you get back," she said. Then she went back to the front gallery to watch us leave, looking like maybe we were going off to die.

I wished Mama wouldn't be like that. Mama was goodhearted about feeding me when I got hungry between meals. She was good to see that I was tucked in snug and warm of a night and was a big comfort when I got hurt. But seemed like she couldn't understand that I just had to get out and prowl the woods sometimes. All she could see for me was schoolgoing and churchgoing and hard work in between times. Fishing, varmint hunting, or just roving the woods to see what I could see—that was a waste of time, the way Mama looked at it. It was the devil himself tempting me to ruination any time I wanted to go.

The dun mare felt good, and we rounded the bend in the lane at a fast trot. A big chicken hawk flew over real low. He screamed at us and spattered a line of white droppings across the wagon sheet covering our camping plunder. Blackie was insulted. He said hold up a minute and he'd learn that smart aleck a lesson. So I hollered "Whoa" to the dun mare and hauled her back in the shafts and Blackie leveled down on the flying hawk with his .22. He cut some feathers out of the hawk's back and scared him into a corkscrew dive.

"Missed!" Blackie said. "But I'll bound you that

booger studies a spell before he messes on the next feller's wagon sheet!" He laughed big and I laughed with him.

I wished I could shoot a gun like that, and guessed maybe I could if I'd had the practice Blackie'd had. I promised myself when we came back with a wagon-load of coon hides to sell, I'd buy me a target gun and a bunch of hulls and smoke up every last one or learn to shoot straight first.

Spud's stuff was lying on the front gallery when we pulled up at his house, but he wasn't ready. He ran to the door and poked his head out and said, "Them girls has stuck my cap away somewhere and I can't find it," and jerked his head back in. And inside, one of his sisters yelled at him: "That's a lie! You lost it yourself!" And Spud said: "It ain't, either. Y'all are always a-primping and cleaning up the place till a body can't lay his cap down nowheres and look to find it again!" And then Spud's mama hollered at them to dry up that fussing and get to hunting. And Spud's baby brother Jiggs set up a howl: "I wanna go, too. I wanna go, too! Mama, lemme go with Spud!"

Spud was my age, but he wasn't skinny and loose jointed like me; he was more chunky and had a rounder face. And he had sandy hair, where mine was so white Papa'd nicknamed me Cotton. Me and Spud both had freckles across our noses. And we both had the same color blue eyes.

Spud was poky as a possum, but he was a dead shot with a sling and had the best melon-thumping ear in the county. On the darkest kind of a night, he could pick a ripe melon the first time.

His little old black feist Snuffy came tearing out from back of the house and barked and fussed at the hounds till Drum finally lost patience and growled at him. That seemed to satisfy Snuffy; he went and curled up by Spud's bedroll.

I got down and loaded Spud's stuff on the wagon and about that time I heard his biggest sister Lottie say, "Here's your old cap, right in the woodbox where you threw it!" And Spud said, "I never put it in no woodbox and you know it!" Then he came through the door putting his cap on and looking red in the face. Behind him tagged Jiggs, jumping up and down and crying, "I wanna go! I wanna go!"

Spud picked up his feist and wheeled on Jiggs. "You git back in the house and shut up!" he hollered. Jiggs ran back into the house, screaming bloody murder. Spud's mama hollered at Spud: "Now, is that any way to talk to your little baby brother?"

"Well, make him dry up!" Spud said. And his mama hollered back at him: "Now, don't you get so biggety, young man. I'll set my foot down and you won't leave this house!" So Spud shut up and came and climbed into the wagon with Snuffy, and I started the dun mare off before his mama did maybe change her mind and not let him go.

"You taking that little old feist along?" Blackie wanted to know.

"He can catch a possum!" Spud said.

"What? That thing catch a possum! Why, his tail's curled up so tight, it's pulling his hind feet off the ground!"

Blackie was just joshing and Spud grinned, but he was sort of hacked. "I guess he ain't much of a varmint dog," he said. "But it's more fun to hunt when I got him along."

"We jump us one of them big river coons," Blackie said, "and he'll straighten that feist's tail out!"

He slapped his leg and laughed at that and I laughed with him. But I knew how Spud felt. It had to be a lot more fun when you had your own dog on a varmint hunt and could listen for his tree-bark off out yonder in the dark woods of a night and could say to the rest: "That's that old Snuffy dog of mine. Guess he's put another'n up a tree!"

I sure did wish I had a dog to take on this hunt.

Even a little old bench-legged curl-tailed feist like Spud's.

"Let's go 'round by that boar's den of mine and pick up some steel traps," Blackie said. "We'll trap 'em and dog 'em at the same time."

So we drove past his log shack and loaded on thirty double-spring coon traps, then cut through old man Wagner's sheep ranch toward the main river road.

The sun climbed higher, warming up things. It was just in the shady places where you could see any frost left. By dinnertime we'd be shucking out of our coats and doing fine in our shirt sleeves. Of course, you never could tell. Like Papa was always saying, nobody but a fool or a stranger ever tried to predict Texas weather. Come daylight tomorrow, it might be blowing a blizzard. I sure did hope the bad spells held off till we'd got in our hunt.

We drove down into the crossing on Comanche Creek. The wagon tires made a loud grinding noise in the coarse gravel. The hounds splashed across the shallow water. Right at the edge of it they struck a hot trail and ran it to a tall pecan tree standing on the far bank. They circled the tree a couple of times to make sure, then Drum reared up on it and went to barking.

"That's meat for dinner!" Blackie said.

Spud's black feist Snuffy yelped like he'd been hit with a stick and jumped off the wagon. He turned a somerset in the water, then tore out for the tree, screeching every jump. Rock and Drum stopped barking and stood and watched Snuffy coming. They couldn't make out what was wrong with him. They hadn't been excited about treeing a squirrel; they'd treed lots bigger game. Snuffy ran around the tree, having fits, jumping high up on the straight trunk and climbing it a ways before he fell back.

"Be dog!" said Blackie. "Practice that little old thing up some and he could save a man hulls. He could climb a tree and drag a man's catch out for him!"

Spud's eyes were shining; he was sure proud about how eager Snuffy was to get at that squirrel.

Blackie handed me his gun when I pulled up the dun mare on the far side of the water. "Let's see what kind of a meat getter you are," he said.

I didn't much want to. I was afraid I'd miss and make a poor showing. But I took the gun and went out and started searching the limbs of the tree.

"Now, just one shot!" Blackie said. "And right in the eye, where it won't spoil the meat!"

I moved slowly around the tree. I kept looking till I located the squirrel lying flat against the bark on a high limb. I raised the gun, but my heart was jumping till I couldn't hold my bead. It wasn't that I hadn't shot a squirrel before; it was just knowing that Blackie was watching and would hooraw me if I missed. I held my breath and tried it again.

I thought I saw the squirrel flinch when I shot, but he just kept clinging to that limb and didn't move.

"By gollies, he's missed!" Blackie said. "Spud, go kill that squirrel before he wastes all my hulls!"

I didn't know why it meant so much, missing that squirrel, but for a second there, I was sure sick. Then I heard something spattering on the leaves and saw it was blood.

"I didn't miss!" I hollered. "I hit him."

I saw the squirrel double up, claw at the limb and come tumbling down. He struck another limb below and clung to it a minute before he fell the rest of the way.

I grabbed him up and held him high out of reach of the dogs. Right in the throat; that's where I'd shot him. That's what made him so slow about dropping. It wasn't an eye shot, but it was pretty good. I hadn't ever shot up over a box of target hulls in my life, and them in different people's guns.

Blackie pulled out his knife to dress the squirrel and that's when Spud all of a sudden jumped up and hollered: "Oh, my gosh! I've left my knife! I got to go back and get it! You can't go off on a hunt without no knife."

"Why, confound it," Blackie said. "It's a couple of miles back to the house. We got knives enough."

"We ain't got *my* knife," Spud insisted. "It's a special kind of a knife. I made it myself." He turned to me. "We can go back, can't we, Cotton?" he begged. "It won't take but a little bit."

I knew about Spud's special knife. He'd made it out of a piece of old saw blade, with a deer's foot for a handle, just like those he'd seen the pictures of in that Western magazine. He'd spent every evening for a month getting it made and had just started learning to throw it, the way the bad border Mexican did in that "Hell on the Rio Grande" story we'd read out behind the barn. I guessed it was pretty bad, all right, going off on a hunt and leaving a knife like that.

"Y'all wait here," Spud said, "and I'll run back afoot."

"Lordy mercy!" Blackie said. "If you've got to have that old knife, take Cotton's mare and go git it. Me'n him, we'll take a turn down the creek here and jump us another squirrel."

We didn't jump a squirrel right away, but we located an armadillo and Blackie showed me a thing

I never would have believed. The dogs had crossed
the creek and were prowling in the live-oak thickets
over there, so they missed him. But we heard him
poking around in the leaves and slipped up quiet to
see if it was maybe a turkey scratching. Then we saw
him and Blackie said: "Slip down to the creek and
bring me a fistful of gravels and I'll show you a good
trick."

I couldn't figure what he could do to an old hard-
shelled armadillo with a fistful of creek gravel, but I
brought them and poured them into the hand he
stuck out at me.

"Now, set down and don't move," Blackie whispered.

We sat down in the leaves. Blackie waited till the
armadillo had his head down and was rooting, then
thumped a gravel at him. It fell short about three
feet, but the armadillo heard it. Up came his head
and he ran to where the gravel had rattled the leaves
and went to sniffing around and digging with his fore-
feet.

Blackie thumped another gravel at him, letting it
fall short. It had barely hit before the armadillo had
pounced on the spot where it had fallen and started
searching.

32

Blackie grinned. "The blind old fool thinks it's bugs a-hopping!" he whispered.

He kept thumping more gravel at the stupid armadillo, leading him right up to us. In no time the rascal was right up to within three feet of us, still hunting that hopping bug.

I held my breath, watching. Couldn't he see us? Couldn't he smell us? How close would he come? He ought to hear us breathing by now.

He was already between Blackie's outstretched feet when he finally got scent of us. He reared up on his hind legs, poking his silly nose this way and that, trying to figure out what he was smelling.

Blackie jacknifed his heels toward him, yelled, and grabbed with both hands. He knocked the armadillo off his feet and caught him up in his arms, but he couldn't hold him. The armadillo clawed Blackie on the neck and whacked him across the face with a whipping stroke of his horny tail. Then he was free and making for his hole in a high-jumping run.

"Watch that scalawag git yonder!" Blackie shouted. "Bet he thinks that's the damnedest bug he ever jumped on."

He felt of the scratch on his neck where a little blood was oozing out. There was a red welt across his face, too; that tail had whacked him hard. "Son of a gun!" he complained. "Ain't even got sense enough to take a joke."

Then he slapped his leg and went to laughing big again, and I sat there in the leaves and laughed with him.

We had three squirrels and a couple of jackrabbits when Spud got back with his hunting knife. Blackie said a catfish just couldn't leave a jackrabbit-liver bait alone to save his life.

Spud pulled his foot-long knife out of his home-made leather sheath.

"Lordy mercy, what a pigsticker!" Blackie said. "You look out with that old thing, now. You'll be jabbing it through somebody."

We drove till dinnertime and ate a cold snack at a spring branch where we could water the dun mare. There was watercress growing along the edges of the stream and we cut some and ate it with our biscuits and slabs of roast pork Mama had sent along. The watercress had a biting peppery taste and sure made good eating out of that cold meat. Rock bit off some of the cress and ate it, too, but with his lips curled back like he didn't think much of the taste. Blackie said dogs made themselves eat green stuff now and then to keep their livers toned up and in working shape. He said foxes and wolves did, too.

He said most of the wild creatures were born knowing things it took people a lifetime to learn.

I knew one thing—that watercress sure beat taking the gall-bitter liver medicine Mama got from McConnel's store every spring.

We'd just crossed Honey Creek when Rock and Drum ran onto a big mustard-colored range bull out in the brush. Nine times out of ten, that old bull would have paid them no more mind than he would a prowling fox, but this was that tenth time and the mean, ornery streak that's in all bulls had this one on the prod. He wheeled and took after the dogs.

Rock and Drum ran. They knew Blackie'd twist their ears if they fooled with anybody's cattle. They loped along, just out of reach of that wicked set of horns, looking back over their shoulders and baring their teeth at the bull. They made it plain that if they'd had the say-so they'd have made a fight of it.

They ran under the wagon and the bull saw us then and stopped in the middle of the road. He went to pawing dust and shaking his horns, daring us to come on.

I didn't like it, and the dun mare didn't, either. She fell back against the singletree and snorted. I said, "Whoa!" And Blackie said, "Dog take it! Looks like that scoun'l is horsin' to pick a scrap!"

He stood up in the wagon and told me to hold the mare while he got down and talked it over with the bull.

I'd rather have tried to drive around, but the mesquites and prickly pear were too thick to get the buckboard through. I held a tight rein on the dun mare and waited.

Blackie hopped to the ground and walked toward the bull. Every step Blackie took made it harder for me to breathe.

"What's he gonna do?" Spud said over my shoulder. Spud's freckles stood out plain on his face. I said I didn't know. And Spud said, "That's a mean-looking bull. Blackie's liable to get hisself kilt!"

And Blackie just kept walking slow toward the bull.

The bull stood and watched him come on, then bowed up with a deep, loud bellow that went right through me.

"All right, ole Paw and Beller!" Blackie said. "If it's a fight you want, here's a-looking at you!"

He dropped down on his all-fours and went to bellowing and pawing up fistfuls of dust and throwing it over his back. Just like the bull.

I got so scared I nearly wet my pants. And Spud, he yelped, "Don't, Blackie! Don't do that!"

The hounds ran out from under the wagon and got on either side of Blackie and bayed at the bull. Blackie hollered for them to get back, but they wouldn't listen. The bull might get Blackie, but not if they could stop him.

The bull shook his head and snorted. Blackie shook his head and snorted.

The bull bellowed and Blackie bellowed right back at him. Pawing together, they had the road dust boiling in the sunlight.

Then the bull's head dropped down and I saw his tail lifting and knew he was fixing to charge. "Run, Blackie! Run!" I hollered.

Then the mad bull came at him, his big feet shaking the ground.

Spud, he yelled: "Run, Blackie!"

And Blackie ran straight at the bull!

He was off his knees now and goat-jumping toward the bull on his hands and feet, his head down and his rump end sticking up high in the air.

The hounds went to meet the bull with him, but they didn't bluff the big devil. It was Blackie, coming straight at the bull, with his butt sticking high in the air, that spooked him. Right at the last second, he snorted and wheeled so fast that he lost his footing. He piled up in a gully beside the road.

The hounds went onto him, roaring and biting him in the face, and Blackie got to his feet in time to run up and give him a hard kick in the tail as he reared up out of the gully. Then the bull was gone in a rattle-hocked run, popping the mesquites as he went. The hounds went with him, baying and snapping at his heels.

Blackie stood at the side of the road and scolded. "Now, plague take it!" he said. "That'll learn you to git ringy with Blackie Scantling! Go find you a green heifer. Then you can git your mind back on your grazing!"

He hollered for Rock and Drum, but they couldn't hear. So he came and climbed into the wagon. He knew they'd come back after a while.

"Whew!" he breathed, flopping down in the spring seat by me. "You know, there for a minute, I didn't think I was going to turn that old scoun'l!" Then he rocked back in the spring seat, laughing at the top of his voice.

Me and Spud, we laughed, too; but ours were sort of weak laughs.

3

AT THE river, we pitched camp under a stand of tall winter-bare elms and pecans that grew out of a dirt bank above the water. If this had been a summer fishing trip, we'd have moved in under the monster live oaks hugging the house-high cliff to the back of us. Those old oaks were never bare; they didn't shed till the young leaves pushed the old ones off in the spring. Their waxy green leaves made cool black shadows on the ground. Right now, though, Blackie pointed out that we could use all the sunshine we could get.

A long deep pool of blue water came to a dead end where the dirt bank sloped away further down. A broad, boulder-littered sand bar held up the water and forced it through a narrow channel against the far bank. There were bigger boulders there and they tore at the swift-running water and made it roar and foam white where it poured over and around them. Blackie said in that shoal water was the place to cane-pole fish for forked-tail channel cats in warm weather.

The rock cliffs stood high on the other side of the river, with only one deep V-shaped break where a creek came through. Above the cliffs were rock-bench slopes, with scrub cedar, catclaw, prickly pear, and bear-grass clumps, all growing in a thorny tangle.

It was such a rough and wild and lonesome-like country that it scared you off and pulled at you to stay, all at the same time. I couldn't unload the wagon for standing and looking. I felt like nobody but God and the Indians had ever been here before.

I knew better than that, of course. Right here was

where Papa and Blackie and Blackie's older brother
Joe had camped the time that old Nigger dog and
the pups had tangled with the bobtailed coon and
fought all over Joe. And just up the creek yonder
and around the bend was where Dave Wilson and
his woman lived with Grandpa and Grandma Wilson. And down in the bend of the river, where the
mouth of that little cave showed black against the
face of the cliff, that was where the wild bees lived
and had been storing away honey for always. One
man had been there before and tried to rob the bees.

"But his nerve didn't hold out," Blackie said,
telling about it again. "There wasn't no way to
climb up from the bottom of the cliff, so he got his
bee-robbing plunder together and tied a rope
round hisself and had some other fellers let him
down from the top. And then he got to thinking:
*What if that rope was to break or them fellers let it
slip?* And be dog if he didn't faint dead off.

"Damned fool was lucky, at that," Blackie wound
up. "If he'd ever got inside that cave and riled them
bees, they'd have stung him to death. Them's them
little old wild black bees, and tampering with them
scogies ain't a paying proposition."

We'd no more than got camp pitched when the
dogs went to baying and we looked up and saw Dave

Wilson riding through the water. He was leading a snorty young bay horse on a new rope hackamore. Beside him, on a gray mule, rode a girl in an old hull of a saddle that had her dress pulled up above her knees. The girl wore a ducking jumper and a man's cap with the bill turned up in front. She had long brown hair that spilled back over her shoulders and sparkled in the sunlight.

Blackie hollered, "Dry up!" at the barking hounds and went out to meet Dave and the girl. Me and Spud went along.

Dave and the girl came on across the river and stopped out in the middle of the rocky bar. Dave had the girl snub the spare horse up to her saddle, then he swung down and started loosening the girth.

Blackie said, "Now I wonder what Dave's fixing to do."

We went down to where the girl held the bay snubbed up close to her saddle horn. Dave was trying to get his saddle on the horse's back. I guess the bay never had had a saddle on him, judging from his shaggy looks and the way he kept snorting and jumping out from under.

Blackie said, "Lordy mercy, you ain't fixing to ride that fool horse out here in this boulder pile, are you? He'll kill hisself and you, too!"

Blackie was talking to Dave when he said it, but he was looking at the girl.

She wasn't a great big girl, but she had long, strong-looking, slim legs, like maybe she'd be fast afoot. She had brown eyes like Mama's, sort of soft and pretty. And you could tell she was used to laughing and showing her white teeth a lot. She was half laughing now and matching Blackie, look for look.

The bay wheeled and kicked at Dave with both hind feet, but Dave just swayed to let the heels whiz past his head. He slapped his saddle square on the horse's back this time. He reached under quick and caught up the loose, flopping girth and said over his shoulder, "Out in these boulders is the place to take the starch out of a salty one. Them slick river rocks, they keep him throwed off balance till he can't pitch so hard!"

He jerked the girth up tight and buckled it, then stepped back to turn and grin at us. "Looking down at them rocks helps me to keep in the saddle, too," he said. "I tell myself: 'Now, Dave, if you let him stack you, the only thing that'll give when you hit will be your own old bones!' So I screw down tight in the saddle and sure hang and rattle."

He winked at me. It didn't make sense to me, him crawling a bad horse down here in these river rocks;

43

but his wink made me feel good. Dave was tough and reckless. You could tell that by the way he wore his Stetson pulled slaunchways across his head and by the bold, laughing look in his gray eyes. But he was the kind that would hunt you up in town of a Saturday to buy you an ice-cream cone. And I guessed you had to be tough to break out wild horses and run a ranch.

Dave nodded his head toward the girl and said to Blackie, "That there's Dony Waller. Sister to my woman, Rachael. She's a ring-tailed tooter, Dony is!"

"You mean old Fiddling Tom Waller's littlest girl?" Blackie asked. He looked surprised. "Why," he said to her, "you wasn't hardly frying size when I swang them girls around at that wedding dance your daddy give for Dave and his woman. How long's that been, Dave?"

"Three year, come April," Dave said.

"I guess I've feathered out some since then," the girl Dony said. She straightened in the saddle and took a deep breath that made her ducking jacket fall apart and show where she swelled to fill out her red sweater. "I might could show you a thing about swing-dancing now!"

"That's a mortal fact!" Dave said. "You never seen a lighter foot!"

44

Blackie didn't say anything to that. He just ran a slow look up and down the girl and back again.

I'd never seen the kind of look that came into Blackie's eyes then. It gave me a funny, kind of uncomfortable feeling, like maybe I didn't really know Blackie, here after I'd known him all my life.

That look must have bothered Dony, too; I saw a blush start crawling up her neck into her face. But she didn't look away from Blackie and she didn't try to cover up her knees, either.

"Well," said Dave. "I ain't going to get the kinks curried out of this bronc just standing here thinking about it. Y'all gimme room; I'll see what sort of a warp he's got to his backbone."

He let me hold his other horse for him and then went and unwrapped the lead rope on the bronc from Dony's saddle horn. He coiled the rope and caught up the cheekpiece of the hackamore and pulled the bay's head around and held it there till he could get a boot in the stirrup and swing up. Then he cut loose with a holler and the bay snorted and went straight up, pawing the air.

Dave yelled again. He jerked off his hat and whipped the bay between the ears with it to bring him back down. The bay bogged his head and went out across the boulder bar, pitching and stumbling and grunting loud.

"Lordy mercy!" Blackie said. "That Dave's going to git his neck broke, messing with them old bad horses."

"I could ride 'em!" Dony said. "I could ride 'em just like Dave if they'd let me."

The way she said it, I couldn't help believe she could, too.

"That ain't for a pretty girl," Blackie said. "That's for damn fools and cowhands. A pretty girl, she wants to frolic and wear silk and cook up fancy eats for some man."

"I can do those things, too!" Dony said, and looked straight at Blackie.

They'd both forgotten me and Spud. And they didn't even see Dave and the pitching horse.

The bay went into the shoal water, splashing it high, and then out of it again. Dave balanced himself up in the saddle, spurring and whooping and whipping the horse over the head with his hat like he didn't care whether he got thrown or not.

Spud said, "Some day I'm going to be a bronc buster."

"Me, too!" I said. If Spud could learn to ride wild horses, I could, too. It would sure be fine to ride a bad horse like that sometime, with folks looking on and being scared to death I'd get hurt; but of course I wouldn't. I'd be too good a rider.

"We'll ride wild horses all the time we're not varmint hunting," I told Spud.

The bay stumbled again and nearly fell, then threw up his tail and quit pitching. Dave spurred him into a hard run and circled us a couple of times, then hauled back on the hackamore. The bay squatted and slid to a halt, showering us with sand and gravel.

"He sure had my old bones rattling there for a little bit," Dave said.

He slipped out of the saddle and gave the panting bay a couple of hard, friendly slaps on the shoulder. The bay snorted, but he didn't dodge. He just stood there, blowing hard and quivering in the flanks and hind legs.

"I can manage now, Dony," Dave said. "You'll be night getting in home like it is." He started loosening his saddle cinch.

Dony lifted her reins and swung her mule around and Blackie said: "You reckon a man could stir out something if he was to come a-hunting down in your part of the country?"

Dony looked back over her shoulder and a half

47

smile showed her white teeth again. "He might,"
she said, then added, "providing he knows how to
go about it!"

She rode off, leaving me with a sort of bother that
I couldn't figure out. I didn't know for sure, but
seemed like she and Blackie both had been saying
one thing and meaning another. Grown people did
that sometimes; I'd caught Mama and Papa at it
more than once.

Dave pulled his saddle off the bay and put it on
his other horse. "Y'all catching any varmints?" he
wanted to know.

"Just got here," Blackie told him. "Guess we'll
dog-hunt on this side of the river and trap on the
other. Don't look to make a big catch. Old dogs ain't
much 'count."

"Well, good luck," Dave told us, putting a foot
into his stirrup and going on up onto his horse.
"Come see us." He waved a hand and rode on off.

Blackie stood for a while, digging at the hole in
his pants and staring off down the river in the direction Dony had ridden her mule.

"Dave oughten to have that little thing helping
him with them old bad horses," he said at last.
"Pretty as she is, a man ought to put her in a picture
frame and keep it setting on his mantelboard, just
to look at."

I followed him and Spud back to camp, with a sort of uneasy, lonesome feeling, like maybe Blackie had gone off somewhere and left us. He hadn't, of course; he was right here with us and we were going to go make some coon sets. But the feeling kept worrying me anyhow.

Judging by the sun, it was four o'clock when we crossed the river on a row of stepping rocks we'd thrown into the water ahead of us. We turned upstream, with Blackie packing his steel traps across his shoulder. Spud and I packed the jackrabbits. We didn't want to make any coon sets on our side of the river, Blackie told us; the fool hounds were liable to get into them.

Blackie watched the varmint trails as we went and me and Spud looked, too, trying to learn to read the sign left by the wild things. We found where coons had been cracking pecans under a tree like range hogs; we set one trap there. Me and Spud gathered dry sticks and Blackie built up a little pen of them against the tree, leaving a gate open. He set the trap in the opening, covering it with light leaves, and left a jackrabbit leg for bait inside the pen.

Further along, Blackie walked out on a sand bar at the edge of the river and picked up three mussel-shell halves, big as your hands.

"Them's real coon bait," he told us, tucking them into his jumper pocket.

Me and Spud were all eyes. There were mussel shells lying all up and down the river. A coon could find one anywhere, but he couldn't eat one after he found it. We couldn't figure how you could trap a coon with a hard mussel shell. But we just looked at one another and kept quiet.

Where the water ran ankle deep over a broad flat-rock bottom, Blackie squatted and pressed down the springs of a trap and set the trigger. He reached the trap out and let it down easy to the bottom where the water just barely covered it. Then he got a drift log and brought it down near the water and wired the trap chain to it. Finally, he got out his mussel shells and washed them till the pinkish silver of their linings shone bright, and set them in a circle around the trap.

"Comes old Coon a-froggin' along here in the moonlight," he said, talking to nobody much. "Eye lights on shine of them shells. Old Coon's curious about play-pretties as a woman. He say: 'Be dog! Wonder what's gatherin' them puddles of moon-shine out there in the water!' And he wade out and get to feeling around to see, and that trap jump and grab him and he fall back and squall at the top of

his voice: 'Confound it! I might a-knowed that
Blackie Scantling was up to his same old tricks!' "

Blackie was squalling just like a mad coon when
he said that last, and it set me and Spud to laughing
till the tears came. After that, we kept on breaking
out with the giggles or starting a brand new laugh
all over again. We felt wild and free, 'way off out
here at the back side of nowhere, a million miles
from schoolbooks and face washings; and learning
to trap for fur and knowing that before morning
we'd have tramped through these hills, hunting with
the hounds.

We couldn't hold it in. We ran and laughed and
hollered. Then we hollered some more because the
cliffs would holler back at us, time and again. We
kept it up till Blackie threatened to throw us in the
river and hold us under.

"Dog take it!" he said, acting real grouchy, "y'all
keep up that racket and you'll run ever' varmint on
the river clean over the county line!"

We hushed then—but it was too late. It was bound
to have been all that hollering that led Ed Waller
right to us.

The sun was getting low and Blackie said we'd
set this one last trap before we turned back. He was
down on his knees setting it when Ed Waller rode

out of a clump of tall cedars and pulled up his big roan horse almost on top of us. He was a big fat man in brush-frayed garments and he wore a wide-brimmed hat sitting square on his head, pulled down low in front. He had a fat face and little mean eyes.

I knew him the minute I saw him. I'd seen him around town of a Saturday, always alone and always watching everybody he passed like he thought they might be trying to put one over on him. He was a hog man and folks called him "Hog" Waller behind his back and said they'd sure want to build the pens high around any fattening hogs they had if they lived neighbors to him.

He said to Blackie: "Who give you permit to set traps on the river here?"

Blackie sat back on the run-over heels of his shoes and frowned up at him. "Why, nobody give me permit," he said. "I ain't asked for none. I've trapped and hunted and fished on this old Dillon Ranch always, and there ain't nobody ever raised a fuss. Why? You bought it?"

Waller spat tobacco juice right at Blackie's feet. "I got hogs running on this river," he said flatly. "I don't want 'em trap-crippled."

"All right," Blackie said. "Keep your hogs at home and they won't git caught in my traps."

A hard shine came into Waller's little eyes. All of a sudden I was scared.

But all Waller did was spit tobacco juice again and wheel his big roan horse around.

"I'll go see Dave Wilson about this," he said. "By God, there's some of us as has to work to get along. We got more to do than prowl the woods like a varmint. And we don't hold with some damned tramp coming along and crippling our stock."

Blackie shrugged. "They's varmints prowling these woods," he said, "that's a damned sight more decent acting than some humans I know."

But Waller didn't hear. He'd already raked the roan with his heavy spurs and taken him down the river bank at a high lope.

Me and Spud weren't laughing and hollering now. Seemed like the river canyon was a lot darker and colder than it had been.

Blackie pulled up his half-set trap, sprung it, and slung it over his shoulder. "There ain't no kind of a bait," he said, winking at us, "that'd lead a respectable coon past where that thing spit his tobacco juice. Let's git back to camp and fix supper."

"You reckon Dave Wilson'll raise a fuss?" I asked. I was a lot more worried than Blackie let on to be.

"Dave's all right," Blackie said. "He won't let that tub of leaf lard worry him none."

Spud said, "What right's Waller got to stir up a stink if he don't own the land? He don't even have no right to run hogs on it."

One corner of Blackie's mouth jerked down. "There's just people like that," he said. "Can't learn to live and let live. Ed Waller's old daddy left him a two-thousand-acre ranch up the river when he died. Well stocked, too. But it ain't enough for Hog Waller. He's one of them what wouldn't be satisfied if he owned a controlling interest in all Creation. He'd still want to crack the whip over the head of the Almighty.

"Lordy! If I had it, I'd think I was richer than the dirt in an old cow pen. Without half working, I could eat fancy, wear fine clothes, drink good whisky, and have all the women I could stand up to. What in hell else is there worth a man's having?"

He stopped to point out the tracks of a big fox in the dust of a cow trail, then added: "Dog take it! I'm proud I never let money git a strangle hold on me!"

The sun hung in a low crotch in the hills and laid a trail of gold down the middle of the river. We crossed on our stepping rocks and Blackie said: "Let's make a couple of bank sets down here at these willers, then go eat supper."

I was still uneasy, but it looked like Blackie'd already shoved Ed Waller out of his mind.

We walked downstream, stumbling over the boulders, to a couple of willows that hung over a slow-moving whirlpool at one side of the shoals.

"Take a big old catfish," Blackie said. "He's lazy as a fat dog. He don't want to git out yonder and wrassle that current for his rations. He'd druther lay in here where it's still and wait for what grub the river'll bring him. Me'n your daddy, Cotton, we hung a regular horse in here once. But he got away."

Out of his jumper pocket Blackie pulled a couple of throw lines wound around sticks. He unwound them down to the hooks and lead sinkers and baited the hooks with jackrabbit livers. Then he tied the free ends of the lines to willow branches and pitched the baits out into the pools where they sank to the bottom.

"Now, let's see a big un break loose," he said. "Them springy willer limbs, they'll whip the starch out of him in a hurry!"

Spud said: "I brung along a bell." He reached into his coat pocket, looking half ashamed to, and pulled out a tom turkey bell. There was a wad of grass inside to keep the clapper quiet. "I heard tell

the leaves and circled two or three times before they curled up on the foot of Blackie's bed. I saw Snuffy come shivering up to Spud's bed and nose around the covers till Spud reached out and drew him under. And I wished again that I had me a dog to come and cuddle up close to me. But it wasn't a real biting wish now, like it had been. My mind was too jumbled up with thinking about what all had happened today and what might happen before morning.

I went through Blackie's fight with the mad bull again and could laugh to myself about it, now that it was all over. Some people would likely say that Blackie had taken a fool risk when there wasn't anything to be gained. And I guessed maybe he had; but it was still a fine thing to have seen. I got a warm feeling, knowing that I had a thing to tell that would make good listening to even grownups.

There was that armadillo trick, too. I could pull that sometime. Anybody could pull that if he knew it. But that was the thing; mighty few people knew it could be done!

I guessed the woods was just working alive with big secrets, if I had the time and somebody like Blackie to teach me. Some day, I promised myself, I'd learn them all. I'd go with Blackie all I could now. And when I got grown, I'd take to the woods, too. Other people could plow in the fields and run grocery stores and blacksmith shops and post offices and build houses to raise families in and go to church and bother with book learning. I didn't aim to waste my time with it any more than I had to.

Blackie was smart. Smarter than Papa, even. Blackie didn't do the kind of living that kept him at home and hard at work all the time. I guessed he was the smartest man I knew. I hoped I could be like that, too, and not let money get a strangle hold on me.

I meant to worry some about what would happen if we caught one of Hog Waller's hogs in our traps. But there were too many good things to think about. I never got around to that.

4

I CAME up out of my warm bed into the dark, shivering with cold and excitement. It was Spud hollering: "The bell's ringing. I hear the bell. We've caught a big fish!" And I knew then that I'd been hearing the bell ring a long time, but just couldn't make myself wake up.

There was the muffled barking of a dog mixed in with the sound of the little turkey bell.

Blackie said: "Roust out of there, Cotton! That's a big un, all right. He's made splash enough for old Rock to hear and go bay him."

I was still trying to cram my feet into my shoes when Spud tore out for the river with a lighted lantern. Blackie was next to go, and I wished I'd slept with my shoes on, like Spud. I couldn't lace them in the dark; so I just lit out with the strings slapping around my ankles.

I caught Spud and Blackie before they reached the river. Spud fell down on the rocks and sent the lantern rolling and Blackie had to stop and light it while Spud got up.

Drum was at the catfish hole and baying loud, time we got there. Spud's Snuffy came running up, too, yipping and whining.

The lantern light shoved back the dark over the pool and we could see the willow branch jerking above the water. Blackie lifted the light higher. Our eyes followed down the tight line to where the water surged and boiled. Then we all stood with our mouths hanging open.

It was old Rock out there on the end of that catfish line, bawling and crying for somebody to come get him off before the current sucked him under.

"Well, I'll just be tee-total damned!" gasped Blackie. "Now, how in the hell . . . Here, hold this

61

light, Cotton. That old fool's just about drownded!"

I held the light and Blackie shucked out of his clothes the fastest I ever saw.

"Lordy mercy, that's going to be cold!" he said and jumped off into the icy water. Blackie started swimming toward Rock and hollered back over his shoulder. "Cut that line, Spud, soon as I git my hands on him!" His teeth were already chattering.

Spud pulled out his big knife and caught up the line and Blackie hollered back, "All right, cut us loose!" Spud whacked the line and the current caught up Rock and Blackie and jerked them out of the circle of light.

I heard a big splash and Blackie yelled "Lordy mercy!" again and then I couldn't hear anything or see anything of them. I started running down the river bank, calling to Blackie. I was scared.

Spud came running after me, moaning: "They're drownin', Cotton! They're drownin'!" Then he fell down again and I fell with him. The lantern went out, and all around us was the dark. We couldn't see Blackie; we couldn't hear him.

"Lordy mercy! Light that lantern and find me my shoes!"

It was Blackie! We could hear him now, scrambling up over those frosted boulders at the bank, his rattling teeth making more noise than the rocks he stepped on.

"Git a move on!" Blackie said. "Time I make it to a fire, all my perticklers will be froze and dropping off!"

Back at camp, we built up a big roaring fire. Blackie stood in his shoes and toasted his naked skin till it was pink and cussed old Rock for going down there after that catfish bait of jackrabbit liver.

Still naked, he squatted by the fire and had me and Spud hold Rock down while he cut the fishhook out of his lip with Spud's homemade knife.

"Now, the thing that's puzzling me," he said, "is how that old fool ever got hold of the bait in the first place. He wouldn't have dove down to the bottom of the catfish hole after it. There's times he don't show no more sense than a red ant in a hot skillet, but he wouldn't a-done that!"

We all sat there and frowned into the fire and wondered how on earth old Rock had managed to get hold of that liver bait under eight foot of water.

Blackie finally tugged at the ducktail curl of hair at the back of his neck. "All I can figure," he said, "something drug that bait out on the bank and Rock got it and then fell in the river."

"Like a turtle, maybe?" I asked.

"I'll bet that's it," Blackie said.

He got to his feet and started putting on his clothes. "Well, anyhow, that's the coldest all-over bathing I've done in many a winter. By rights, I oughta cave that old Rock dog's head in with a club."

I wished Mama could have seen how quick Blackie had jumped in to save old Rock. Or even how brave he'd been, chasing the bad bull off. I guessed she'd see that he wasn't just a no-account, fiddle-footed rake. She'd see that he was a real noble man!

A big fat moon started humping up back of the ridge, shooting long bars of gold into the canyon. The river shone silver where the water was still, but down in the shoals the water was smoking. In the pale light the trees and cliffs looked like the black paper cutouts we'd made in school once for Hallowe'en.

Blackie said: "A boar coon that wouldn't prowl on a night like this is laid up with a broke leg. Let's give 'em a round."

"You guess old Rock can make it?" Spud asked. "He looks mighty wore out and shivery."

"He'll warm up," Blackie said. "He brung it on hisself!"

We headed downriver, with Blackie glancing up

to the right and then to the left, getting himself located by the stars. Around us circled Spud's feist, sniffing under logs and rocks and shoving his nose into every armadillo hole he came to. If Snuffy had ever even scented a coon, Spud and I didn't know about it.

"Likely we're going wrong," Blackie said. "Likely we oughta headed for them high ridges back up the river."

"Well, let's go back, then," Spud said. "Let's us go to the best place."

Blackie took another look at the stars. "Aw, you never can tell. Liable not to catch nothing back up in there, nuther. We'll head for them big post-oak bottoms down below."

Eager as I was to go, any place suited me. On a real coon hunt like this, all I wanted to do was get started.

The hounds watched Snuffy working hard at finding mice and armadillo holes. But they finally decided he didn't know what it was all about and drifted off into the brush.

A mile down the river, we heard old Drum open. "*Coooooon!*" he said, in that big drum-sounding voice of his. He said it again, just as plain: "*Coooooon!*" And down in the river canyon, the cliffs picked up his voice and said it after him. *"Coooooon! Coooooon! Coooooon!"* And then old Rock joined him, his high clear voice setting the cliff echoes to ringing like church bells of a Sunday morning. I couldn't remember ever hearing such a stirring sound in my life.

Snuffy tore out toward them, yelping and squealing.

"They've started one!" hollered Spud.

Blackie shook his head and led off in a trot. "Them mush-headed old fools," he growled.

"What's the matter, Blackie?" I asked. "What's happened?"

"Why, confound them clabber-mouthed idjits!" he said. "They've gone and picked up the back end of that coon trail. They're going in the direction he come from. Knowed it the minute old Drum opened his head."

"But if he knows enough to bark different when he's on the wrong end of the trail," I asked, "why doesn't he turn around and take the right end?"

"That's a fool hound-dog for you!" Blackie said. "I'll take them old devils to a good selling one of these days." He lifted his voice and called sharply. "You Drum! Rock! Come back here, you old devils!"

Rock and Drum came back with their tails tucked, looking mighty shamed.

They stood and cringed while Blackie said, "Now, confound it, git out yonder and take the right end of that coon trail." Then they straightened up and loped off up a ridge and circled a lightning-struck post oak a time or two. And when they led off in the opposite direction this time, even I could tell the difference in their voices. They were on the right end of that coon trail now and they were taking it yonder.

Blackie hurried ahead, calling for me to light the lantern. I lit it and rushed to where he knelt on the ground beside the dead post oak. I held the light close and there in the loose sand of a gopher mound was a big coon track. The biggest one Blackie said he'd ever seen.

Blackie got up, shaking his head. "We'll never take the rind off a big boar coon like that now," he grumbled. "With the lead they let him git on us, he'll leave us so fast it'll look like we're backing up."

But he didn't call in the dogs. He led off at a swinging trot in the direction they were going and me and Spud lit out after him.

The trail led over the ridge and down into a dry wash on the other side. Then it cut back toward a creek bottom. We trotted after the dogs. Blackie crippled along through the frosted grass like his trash-pile shoes hurt his feet.

It was a fast run, and a long one. That old coon had his bag of tricks, like Blackie'd said all the smart ones have, and he opened it on this chase. He marked a tree every hundred yards or so. He crossed and recrossed a shallow-water creek. He ran the top of a slab-rock fence, circled boulder piles, back-tracked himself, and once climbed a ragged-faced rock cliff too steep for the hounds. They'd had to hunt a gentler slope before they could reach the top.

Those were all good tricks, but they were wasted on Rock and Drum. Blackie had shamed Rock and Drum back there at the start and now they aimed to show him what they could do.

"Cooon! Cooooooooon!" Old Drum's deep voice had the frosty air quivering. And above it, Rock's bell baying rang high and clear. Now and then, far behind the hounds, the yelping of Spud's feist Snuffy came back to us. It wasn't Snuffy's fault he couldn't run the coon trail as fast as the hounds. He was trying.

"Lordy mercy! Now, ain't they talking to him!" Blackie said. "That howl of old Drum's, it'll jar the acorns out of a tree." He looked behind. "Come on, Spud!"

"You're going too fast!" Spud puffed. "I can't keep up."

Blackie shortened his steps and we ran slower for a while. Spud gained a little, then began to fall back again. "I tell you," he complained, "you're going too fast!"

"We got to hump it!" Blackie said. "We'll lose them hounds if we don't hump it."

He picked up speed, still crippling along like it hurt him; but he sure covered the ground. I ran with him, the voices of those hounds calling me on. I hated to run off and leave Spud, but I couldn't hang back and take a chance on getting lost from the hounds.

"Plague take it, I wish these old shoes would quit pinching my feet!" Blackie grumbled as we ran. "I'd been laying off to buy me a pair of hunting shoes, but I ran onto these down at the dump ground and it looked like such a waste to pay out good money for new shoes when these didn't have but a couple of little bitty holes in the bottoms!"

The frost had been biting my toes and fingers when the chase started. But now they were plenty warm and I could feel a trickle of sweat running down my backbone. My breath was all gone and the blood pounded in my ears till I could hardly hear. And still the hounds kept going.

"Y'all are still going too fast!" Spud panted.

I looked back. We'd been running fast for ten or fifteen minutes and Spud was still just fifty yards behind.

He was that same distance behind and still complaining when the ringing trail cries of the hounds stopped all of a sudden. There was a silence, then we heard the short choppy barking of both hounds.

"Treed him!" said Blackie, then grumbled, "Be dog if it ain't about time. Confounded old dogs! Run a man off his feet, putting one old coon up. Oughta had him treed thirty minutes ago."

Blackie was proud of the way Rock and Drum had treed the coon; but it wouldn't have looked good to brag, so he grumbled instead.

The coon had taken to a stooping live oak that stood on the bank of the little creek about fifty yards from the river. Rock sat on his rump beneath it, telling the whole world they had a coon up. Drum stood on the other side of the tree, whining and wringing his tail.

We came running up and started circling the tree. The moonlight was bright, but we couldn't see a thing in those thick leaves.

"Coon couldn't find a bare tree to climb," Blackie fussed. "Had to go pick one you can't see a thing in."

We stopped and lit the lantern. Spud came trotting up, all out of breath.

"Y'all run too fast!" he panted. "I couldn't keep up!"

Blackie held the lantern high while we searched the tree for eyes.

"You'll have to watch close," Blackie said. "Some of them old smart ones, they'll cup their hands over their eyes to keep them from shining."

"There they are!" Spud said.

I looked and saw a pair of eyes gleaming like live mesquite coals in the leaves.

"Where?" Blackie said.

"'Way up in the top," I said and pointed.

"Then there's two of 'em," Spud said. "The eyes I seen was down about the first fork!"

"But we wasn't running two coons!" Blackie said. "You can't run two coons as fast as we run this one. Two coons cross each other's trails and mess the hounds up too much."

"Well, there's two coons up this tree," Spud said. "I seen both their eyes just then!"

Blackie was bothered. "Well," he said, "we'll have to shoot one and jump the other'n out to the dogs. Bring me the gun, Spud."

"Gun!" Spud said. "Cotton, didn't you have the gun?"

"I had the lantern," I said. "You said you'd pack the gun."

Spud stared off up at the moon and didn't say anything.

"Dog take it!" Blackie said. "You'd go off and leave your head if it wasn't screwed on! Now, we're in a pickle for sure. Jump one coon out, and the other'n will quit the tree and run off while the dogs is fighting the first un." He stood and pulled at his ducktail a minute and then started gouging his finger around in that hole in his pants. "Well, that's the way it goes," he said.

He walked up to the tree and put his ax down and started feeling for handholds. "Git you some clubs and git set," he said. "Maybe we can handle 'em both, but I sure have my doubts."

We hunted around under the trees for dead branches to use as clubs. I was sure put out with Spud. Seemed like he never could remember a thing.

Blackie started climbing, straining and grunting, dragging off bark and leaves that rattled down out of the tree. The hounds backed off, ready to make the catch. Me and Spud, we spaced ourselves between the hounds.

Blackie climbed higher. I could feel the blood pounding my ears again, the way it had on that long run. I was trembling all over. Anything could happen! This was the thing I'd dreamed about a thousand times. A big coon up a tree—two big coons! And the fight ready to start!

I gripped my club tight and waited. I didn't aim for either of those coons to get away.

"Here's the first un!" Blackie called down. "Leave him to the dogs. It's the other'n that'll git away if we don't stop him."

He thrashed around in the branches and hollered, "Look out!" A black form dropped out of the tree with a shrill yelp. The hounds came roaring in and tied onto it, and we heard a scared screeching above their growling and snarling.

Spud shouted, "That's my feist, Snuffy! That was Snuffy up that tree! That ain't no coon!" Up in the top of the tree we heard a loud squall, then Blackie hollered, "Here comes the other'n!" And a limb split with a splintering crack. Blackie hollered "Lordy mercy!" and came crashing down out of the tree.

He hit the ground on his all-fours in a spot of moonlight and a big, mad, fuzzed-up coon landed beside him. The coon snarled and slapped Blackie in the face.

I swung at the coon, missed, and broke my club square in two against the side of Blackie's head.

Blackie rolled over, flat of his back and squalled, "Lord god almighty, you've broke my jaw!" And

73

Spud screamed, "They're killing my Snuffy, Blackie!" And he went to beating the hounds to make them quit tearing Snuffy apart. And I was so flustered and scared, I just stood there with the stump of my broken club in my hand and watched the big coon take out down the creek bank in a humpbacked run.

Blackie rolled to his feet and grabbed up his ax. He hollered: "He's gittin' away. Stop him before he gits to the river!" And he took out after the coon, calling "Hyar, Rock! Hyar, Drum!" I took out after Blackie.

But Rock and Drum didn't come. They couldn't hear Blackie calling; they were howling too loud from the clubbing Spud was giving them. They were still trying to shake that Snuffy feist dog to death. In the mix-up, they still thought the first thing Blackie had poked out of that tree was a boar coon.

Blackie outran me and caught up with the coon first. He swung his ax up and took a cut at the varmint, but missed, and the coon got a head start again and ran faster than ever.

That was sure a race, there in the white moonlight, with Blackie just barely catching up with the coon, then swinging at him and missing and then running to catch up again. I ran as hard as I could, still gripping my broken club and praying I'd get close enough to use it. But I never did.

Then they were right on the bank of the river, where a rock ledge overhung a deep hole of water. The coon was just going over the ledge when I saw the blade of Blackie's ax flash in the moonlight.

Blackie struck and I heard the coon squall and then heard the splash of him hitting the water. Blackie yelled, "Lordy mercy!" and I saw that he'd swung too hard and lost his balance. He went off the ledge right behind the coon and knocked water high.

I ran hard and got there in time to see Blackie come to the top. Just the other side of him, in another circle of spreading silver rings, was the coon. He acted sort of addled, but he was still able to swim. He was headed for the black shadows on the other side of the river.

"Yonder he goes, Blackie!" I hollered and pointed.

Blackie rolled over in the water and made for the addled coon, swimming with one hand and holding to the ax with the other. He pulled up close and struck with his ax again.

But he couldn't hit hard in swimming water. He couldn't get a brace for his feet. All his lick did was make the coon mad again. The coon snarled and turned on Blackie, and Blackie sure had to do some fast swimming to keep the coon off his head. That old coon was ready to eat him up alive.

Blackie made it to shallow water just in time. The

coon was right on him and Blackie was swimming flat
of his back, keeping the varmint kicked off with his
feet. When his hand touched bottom behind him, he
stood up suddenly in knee-deep water.

The coon whirled to make a quick getaway. But
he wasn't fast enough. Blackie swung his ax high
and the water spilled from it in a silver spray. He
struck, once, a good solid lick.

Blackie dragged the dead coon out of the water.
He held it up by its tail. "Biggest boar coon I ever
seen!" he said. His teeth were chattering.

Spud came running up, hugging Snuffy inside his
coat. Snuffy was still whimpering and Spud was
snuffing loud. Behind him came Rock and Drum,
sneaking along like they'd just been caught stealing
meat out of a smokehouse.

They came up and sniffed the dead coon, then
looked up at Blackie.

Blackie didn't say a word. He just looked at them,
and both dogs tucked their tails and slunk off. They
were sure embarrassed about mistaking Spud's tree-
climbing feist for a coon. They went off 'way out
yonder and stood and whined. Even after we'd got a
fire built, they still wouldn't come up to warm, the
way hunting dogs generally will of a cold night. They

just stood out there and shivered and whined and looked sad. They were waiting for Blackie to let them know it was all right again.

But Blackie wouldn't notice them. He stood and looked up at the stars. "If this keeps up," he said, "I'll be washing up as regular as them town bankers." A chill shook him from head to foot and he moved closer to the fire and the steam boiled up white out of his clothes.

"Dog take it," he grumbled. "We'd a-done better to've headed for them high ridges back up the river, like I said the first time. Never did figure we'd do much good down here in these post-oak bottoms."

Me, I was satisfied. I was out of breath and worn down to a nub. Spud's feist had got chewed up pretty bad, and Blackie had taken another wetting in that cold river water. But we'd caught us a big boar coon!

5

SUNUP was just a couple of minutes back of the ridge behind us when we dropped off down into the river canyon and walked through the live-oak mott into camp. I was half asleep on my feet and Spud was fifty steps behind, packing Snuffy and complaining that we walked too fast; so it was Blackie who saw the hogs.

He said, "Confound the luck! Looky yonder!" And I woke up and looked; a whole bunch of range sows and shoats were rooting in our beds and gobbling up our grub and scattering our camp stuff all over creation.

Blackie started running through the live oaks, hollering, "Sooee!" and "Sic 'em, Rock!" and "Git the hell out of here, you plague-taked wretches!" He stopped quick, bent over, and came up with a fist-sized rock that he sent humming into the bunch. A shoat squealed and ran in circles, holding up a crippled leg. The hounds rushed in, baying loud and savage, and the old sows all ganged up with their rump ends against a rock ledge and went to fighting the dogs.

They were sure vicious looking, those old range hogs. Long and thin as fence rails, with their bristles up and their tusks bared; they made a scary sound with their roaring and teeth popping.

But Blackie grabbed up a club and waded right into them, beating the hogs in the face, backing them slowly out of camp. Now and then, one of the sows would get up the nerve to charge him. She'd come at him with a coughing roar, cutting high and fast with her white tusks. And Blackie would stand in his tracks till the last second, then jump straight up and throw his legs apart and let her run between them.

I wanted to help Blackie before one of those hogs got him, but I couldn't make my legs move. They just wouldn't do it. All I could do was stand there, frozen, listening to the squealing and baying and hollering. Then, to one side, I heard the dun mare snorting. She'd got spooked at the uproar and had fallen back against her tie rope, trying to break loose. I ran to get hold of the rope and quiet her. My legs would work, going to the mare. I was ashamed that they wouldn't take me toward those fighting hogs, and I hoped Blackie wouldn't notice, but I couldn't help it.

Spud didn't go in there, either. He stood off and hollered and threw rocks. His Snuffy feist jumped out of his arms and ran and tied right into a big shoat. Snuffy caught the shoat in the ear and led him off, squealing loud, and you could tell Spud was mighty proud about it. But Spud kept clear of the fight himself.

I guess I'd have thought to throw rocks pretty quick if I hadn't had to go to the mare. But I couldn't afford to let her get away and maybe run off and leave us all afoot, 'way down here on the river. So I held to her and said, "Whoa, Dun! Take it easy!" till she quieted down, then kept holding onto her so Blackie would see what had kept me from siding him and the hounds in the hog fight.

At the end of the ledge, the tight front of the hogs finally broke. They turned tail and took to the brush, throwing the fight to us. Blackie hurled his club at the last one and let the dogs chase them on off.

Just then, an old big sandy-colored sow that had been up in the wagon all the time jumped out, a whole side of bacon clamped in her mouth.

Spud saw her and said, "No, you don't!" and grabbed a frying skillet and started beating her over the head. She squealed like he was killing her and headed in a blind run for the river bank. But she didn't drop the meat.

Blackie hollered, "Lordy mercy, Spud, save that side of bacon. It's all we got!" And Spud ran beside the sow and kept beating her with the skillet till he hung his toe under a root and rolled in the leaves. Time he could get up, she'd got too big a lead on him; so he did just like that bad border Mexican in the "Hell on the Rio Grande" story. He jerked his knife out of the scabbard and brought it up over his head and flung it.

That bad Mexican never made a better throw.

81

The knife turned over in the air just once and drove in almost to the hilt down beside the backbone. The sow sure did squeal this time, and Spud threw us a look back over his shoulder that was mighty full of pride.

But he hadn't stopped the sow. She went right off the bank into the water, taking Spud's knife with her. And still holding onto that bacon, too. Spud, he stood there with all the proud look going out of his face, and watched her strike out for the other side, swimming fast.

Then Spud started jumping up and down and hollering, "My knife! She's packing off my knife!" And Blackie came down and stood beside him and said, "Now, wouldn't that pop your eyeballs!" And the sow went swimming on off with her rump end sinking lower and lower. The knife sank out of sight, and then all of the hog's back, and finally there wasn't anything showing except the side of bacon moving off across the river and leaving a V-shaped wake in the water.

The knife was still in the sow when she went out on the far bank. We could see the handle wobbling every step she took toward the brush. And she still had that side of bacon, too.

Spud stood gulping and swallowing like it was

hard for him to get his breath. I could tell that his tear bucket was brim full and fixing to slop over, so I turned away to keep him from knowing I knew.

Blackie saw how it was with Spud, too, and slapped him on the back and said: "Well, dog take it, the old fool's got to have a knife to slice that bacon with, ain't she?" And he slapped his leg and went to laughing, and I acted like I thought it was a good joke, too, and Spud swallowed and managed to hold it. He came on back and was the first one to start picking up the mess the hogs had made of our camp.

They'd sure wrecked it, all right. They'd rooted and trampled our beds with muddy feet and eaten all our salt and scattered a sack of flour all over the place. They'd even tried to bite into the cans and jars holding the other stuff. I found the sack that had held the candy Mama sent along, but we never found hide nor hair of the dozen eggs that'd been in a pasteboard box. Or the box, either. Blackie said he guessed they'd eaten box, eggs, and all. He said a range hog would eat anything. He claimed they'd get to where they'd catch and eat newborn calves or lambs or kid goats.

"Why, 'way back yonder one time," he said, "there was some folks living up on the San Saba and they had a little bit of a baby girl just able to walk. And she got off out from the house apiece and crawled into an old holler-log salt trough and went to sleep. And a big old wild bar' hog, he come and caught her and went packing her off down the river.

"The woman, she heard the little thing scream and she run out and grabbed up a chopping ax and run the hog down and liked to have chopped him in two with that ax.

"She saved the baby, and it wasn't really hurt a-tall, seeing's how that bar' hog hadn't bit it, only just grabbing up a mouthful of its clothes. But the little thing got all bloody from the cut in the hog and the woman had to take it down to the river and git it washed up and after that she never would eat hog meat again. The woman, I mean. The baby, she et it fine. I guess the little thing was too young to recollect."

Blackie said he didn't guess there was a woman living today handy enough with a chopping ax to've killed that bar' hog without cutting her own baby in two.

"After Ma told me about that, I ain't had a lick of use for ary old range hog. There ain't nothing viciouser in the woods!"

Blackie told us another good story his ma had told him, about that same hog-chopping woman, while we cleaned up camp. It was how one night she fought off singlehanded a bunch of Apache Indians. While they were trying to hack down the barred doors with their tomahawks, she climbed up into the attic with a pot of scalding water and poured it down all over them.

"The way she told it to Ma," Blackie said, "them murderin' red heathen left out of there like cats shot in the tail with bootjacks, screeching and yelping ever' jump, and with the steam rolling up off their naked hides like meat hogs scalded for scraping. Blinded some of 'em, that hot water did, and they'd run right head-on into a pole fence or a tree and knock their fool selves down and then they'd git up and run into something else. She said one of 'em ran into a tied-up kicking mule, and that long-eared booger snorted and wheeled around and kicked the Injun plumb over a seven-foot branding corral fence."

Time Blackie finished talking, it seemed almost worth it, having the hogs raid our camp, just to get his recollections stirred. Spud must have felt the same way about it, too, because before we were done, all the hurt about losing his knife was gone out of his face and he was asking questions as fast as I was.

For a little bit I was worried about losing so much of our rations. I was scared we might have to go in home or something. But Blackie wasn't bothered.

"A man can always shoot his meat," he said. "And if that piece of a sack of flour don't last, we'll go borrow from Dave Wilson."

We rustled a batch of breakfast and ate it and Blackie told us to turn in and sleep while he went to run our trap line.

I argued about that. I was so tired I ached in every bone, and now that my stomach was full I could just barely hold my eyes open. But I argued anyhow. I told Blackie we were all partners on this hunting trip and me and Spud aimed to do our part. He said, though, that growing boys needed more sleep and rest than a man did, and I was sure glad. I'd have gone to run those traps to keep Blackie from knowing how played out I was. But nothing else would have made me.

I went to my bed in the leaves and leaned over to lie down and never knew when my face hit the blankets.

The barking of the dogs woke me up. Then I heard the popping and splashing of iron-shod hoofs in the river crossing and sat up quick in bed, half afraid it was Hog Waller coming back to raise another fuss with us about trapping where he ran hogs.

But it was just Dave Wilson riding through the

water. He had that same bay horse on a lead rope, and this time the girl Dony wasn't with him. I was glad of that.

Blackie shut the dogs up and drove another nail into the coon hide he was stretching, raw side out against the trunk of a pecan tree. Then he hollered a loud hello at Dave, and Dave hollered back and the hounds barked louder than ever and went running out to meet Dave.

Spud sat up in his bed and said, "Dad gum, Blackie! You get another coon?" I looked and saw the hide of another coon stretched on the other side of the tree.

Blackie said, "Yeah. Caught him in that water set where I baited with mussel shells. Caught another'n, too, and one ringtail. But them danged old hogs et 'em out of my traps. By rights, a man ought to take his gun and shoot ever' one of them hogs between the eyes." There was a faint blue spot showing under the whiskers on Blackie's jaw. That's where I'd hit him with the club in that coon fight last night.

Dave tied his horses to the willows at the lower edge of the gravel bar and put a rawhide hobble on the forelegs of the dun.

It was the middle of the afternoon now. We'd slept hard ever since sunup. Me and Spud, that is. I wondered if Blackie had slept any; he didn't look sleepy now. I felt fine. I was pretty sore and stiff from last night's hunt and felt a little guilty about the bruise on Blackie's jaw, but Blackie seemed to have forgotten all about it. I guess it wasn't paining him any, so I didn't bother to mention it.

Me and Spud got up and we all went down to watch Dave make his ride. But it wasn't much of a show this time. The bay didn't pitch like he had before. Just sort of goat-jumped a time or two and then lined out into a straight run.

In a little bit, Dave brought him back to where we sat on the rocks, watching. "Smart horse," he said, patting the bay's neck. "Knows when his bluff's been called. Couple more saddles and he'll do for a woman to ride."

Blackie shook his head. "I'll still stick to coon hunting," he said. "I don't take no stock in riding them old bad horses."

"Aw, there ain't nothing to horsebreaking," Dave said. "All it takes is a strong back and a weak mind." He winked at me and Spud. "What luck you have last night?"

Blackie told him about the coon we'd caught and how he'd wound up in the river with him. Dave's eyes got wide.

"You mean," he said, "that you went into swimming water with a mad boar coon? Fan my britches! You couldn't hire me to do that with a wagonload of money!"

It was funny that a man who'd mount and ride a bad pitching horse like Dave had would be scared of water; but he sure was.

Dave said: "Hog Waller come down to the house last night with some wild-haired notion of having me run you boys off; but I ain't got around to it yet." He grinned.

Blackie told him that he hadn't troubled to ask about coming. "Just taken it for granted," he said.

"Why, hell!" Dave said. "You knowed you was welcome. Confound Waller, anyhow! A man's a fool to fight with his neighbors, but I'll be damned if I ain't getting me a full bait of the way Hog'll run his stuff on you and then prize up hell when it ain't protected."

"I lost a couple of furs to them old hogs of his last night," Blackie complained. "And this morning we caught 'em raiding our camp."

Dave frowned and wanted to know if they'd cleaned us out of grub, but Blackie told him we'd make out if we could maybe trouble him for a little biscuit flour, and Dave said sure, he'd be glad to oblige.

"Come on up to the house and we'll get it now," he said.

Blackie shook his head. "We want to make a couple more water sets for coon," he said, "and bait out another catfish line. We'll come later."

Dave said then for us to come up to supper, but Blackie said no, that'd just mis-put his woman, and Dave said it wouldn't a-tall, and that his grandpa would be real tickled to hear about that coon fight in the water, and Blackie said, well, if it wouldn't put them all out too much; so Dave said they'd be looking for us and rode off.

6

IT WAS late when we finished our trap setting. We came back to camp and turned the dogs loose. The river canyon was filling with blue shadows. Already the frogs were tuning up for the night. We headed for the river crossing and supper at Dave Wilson's.

Overhead a long V of redhead ducks shot upriver.

They made the air whistle. Up that high, the last light of the sun struck them from the underside, setting their breast feathers afire.

I walked, not looking where I stepped, watching those fast-flying ducks. Then something happened, and I wasn't Cotton Kinney any more. I wasn't tied down to the earth and stumbling over a heap of river boulders. I was a redhead duck, high in the air, traveling with the speed of a cannon ball.

I could feel the clear cold wind in my face. I could hear the swishing whistle of the air whipping past my wings. I could feel the last warm light of the setting sun on me, turning my breast feathers to gold. And 'way, 'way down below me, I could see the silver streak of the river running between brown canyon walls. And out across a rocky gravel bar I could see the little dark figures of a man and two boys and three dogs, walking along. One of the boys had his face turned up like he was watching and wishing he could come along. But I was flying faster and faster and faster!

Then a man came spurring out of the willows on a big roan horse and hollered "Hey, you! Hold up there a minute!" The dogs went to barking, and I wasn't a fast-flying redhead duck any more. I was **Cotton Kinney** walking through the boulders with

Spud and Blackie and the dogs. And yonder came Ed Waller riding his big roan horse through the boulders at a hoof-popping run, cutting us off from the river crossing.

He hauled the big roan back on his heels right in front of us, Ed Waller did, and piled his fat body out of the saddle. He started our way, swearing as he came. In his hand he held a long-bladed knife with a deer-foot handle.

Me and Spud and Blackie all stopped, then started backing up, leaving the baying dogs in front of us.

"You needn't back off!" Ed Waller shouted at us. "You just as well stop and face it!"

Little cold chills ran up my backbone. But Spud wasn't scared—or else he didn't show it. He spoke up sharp. "That's my knife," he said. "I made it, and it's mine."

Ed Waller cussed Spud. "You don't have to tell me whose knife it is," he said. "What I want to know is how come it stuck up in the back end of the best sow I've got, bleeding her to death."

"Now, take it easy, Hog," Blackie said. "There ain't no call for trouble here."

Ed Waller's angry face grew black. "No call for trouble!" he shouted. "Hell's fire! You stob a knife like this into the back end of the best sow I've got, and then claim there ain't no call for trouble!"

He started toward Blackie, gripping the knife in his hand.

The dogs barred his way, barking and growling savagely. The dogs had their teeth bared and their hair standing up in ridges along their backbones. Ed Waller looked down at them and stopped.

"Call them dogs off," he ordered Blackie. "I'll show you there's call for trouble. I'll show you what it's like to git stobbed in the back end."

Spud's face went gray as ashes. Spud *was* scared. But he started toward Ed Waller. "That's my knife," he said. "I made it and I want it back."

"Come back, Spud," I warned.

But Spud wouldn't listen. "That's my knife," he said. "I made it and I aim to have it back."

Ed Waller looked at Spud. "Git away from me, kid," he warned, "before I slap you flat of your back."

"Now, hold on, Ed," Blackie said. "You can't go around beating up on little old kids over a fool hog. You start doing that, and you'll stir up bad trouble."

"Damn you!" Waller shouted. "The trouble's done stirred up. Ain't nobody can stob a knife in the back end of the best sow I've got and git away with it!"

Spud kept walking toward Waller. He was walking slow, but he kept walking.

"Now, I told you once, kid," Ed Waller said. "You git to messing with me and I'll just sure slap hell out of you."

"I just want my knife," Spud said.

He went on past the barking dogs, walking right up to Ed Waller. Waller backed up a step or two, still gripping the knife in his right hand. He drew back his left hand, and Blackie said sharply: "Now, don't you hit that boy, Hog!" He reached down and picked up a rock.

The hounds and the black feist moved up with Spud, baying louder than ever. Spud said, "Just gimme that knife. I made it and it's mine and I want it back!"

Waller's voice was ugly: "I'll give you hell!" And he slapped Spud down.

The lantern in Spud's hand clattered among the boulders.

The dogs charged Waller with a roar, and above it I heard Blackie's angry yell. The rock Blackie had picked up came whizzing past my head and caught Ed Waller in the ribs. It knocked him off balance and made him stumble in the rocks. The snarling Drum leaped with bared teeth to grab him in the face, but

95

missed and caught him by one shoulder instead, dragging him to the ground. Rock and the screeching Snuffy feist piled on, grabbing holds where they could and shaking and growling.

Ed Waller came up from under the dogs, roaring mad, beating the dogs with his fists. He looked up and saw Blackie coming at him with the ax in his hand. Waller's little pig eyes got big and round. He bawled at the top of his voice, "Don't you hit me, Blackie Scantling!"

He turned and ran, with the snarling dogs slashing at his legs above his boot tops. Blackie ran after him with the ax.

Waller ran straight for his horse. But all the commotion was too much for the big roan; the horse snorted and wheeled away. Ed Waller bawled at him, "Whoa! Damn you, whoa!" He fell to his knees in the rocks and screamed, "My God, don't kill me, Blackie!" and bounced to his feet again.

But he was down long enough for the screeching Snuffy to grab the hold he wanted. And when Waller came to his feet, running hard, he had Snuffy hung to the seat of his pants. Snuffy hung there with his teeth set, his black body swinging down and flopping against Waller's legs every step.

The sight of Snuffy hanging to the seat of Waller's pants broke the mad on Blackie. He stopped and let his ax flop to the ground. He leaned his weight on the handle and started laughing.

He laughed till you could have heard him a mile. But Ed Waller didn't see anything funny. He was running too fast and cussing that spooked roan, and hollering when the hounds bit him, and squalling back at Blackie not to kill him with that chopping ax.

Snuffy hung with his hold, growling and trying to shake it like he had hold of a boar coon. All he could shake, of course, was his own body, and he shook that plenty hard. He was still hanging on and shaking when the big roan finally stepped on the trailing bridle reins and stumbled to his knees. He got up and stepped on the reins again and stopped.

Ed Waller went up into the saddle without touching a stirrup. Snuffy was slung loose. He hit the ground and jumped up and bit the horse on the leg. The big roan snorted and kicked out with both hind legs. Then he took off up the bed of the river, running like a scared wolf. The dogs ran after him, baying loud.

Blackie was past laughing by this time. He was down on his knees. He was still propping his weight up on the handle of his ax while he bent over and grunted and groaned and shed tears like a man bad hurt. His shoulders shook.

Finally he looked up and took a long breath and said, "Lordy mercy! I been all over creation and back and never seen the beat of that!" He bent over and went to grunting and groaning again.

Spud, he got up off the ground and went and picked up his knife where Ed Waller had dropped it when the dogs jumped him. Spud got out his nose rag and wiped off the knife from one end to the other before he stuck it in his scabbard. He said: "He didn't have no right to try to keep my knife!" Spud was still pale.

Up the river, the hounds quit chasing Ed Waller and his runaway horse. They started back in a sweeping, high-tailed trot that kept Snuffy running hard to stay up with them. Blackie got to his feet and swung the ax over his shoulder. "If that don't break that blowhard from sucking eggs, I can't think of nothing that will." He dragged his sleeve across his face to wipe off the tears and headed for the river crossing, still laughing.

Out in the middle of the river, I heard the whistle of wings again. I looked up. It was another V of wild ducks winging upriver. I stood on a stepping rock and watched them. I tried to leave myself and go with them like I'd done with the first bunch, but it was no good this time. The ducks just flew on off and left me standing there.

We walked up the road where the canyon walls stood close and high on each side of the creek, shutting out the fading light. Big live-oak trees grew against the foot of the walls; the oaks leaned out over the creek, making it darker than ever. There were owls in those live oaks. We could hear their booming hoot up ahead. When we got closer, they hissed at us and fell out of the tree tops and spread their wings and went sailing off down the creek toward the river. Their wings made no sound.

Those hoot owls made it ghostly down in that deep canyon. It gave me a creepy feeling, like maybe a panther or something might be fixing to jump out and grab me. But the sound of the creek water pouring over the ledges and through the rocks was a good sound. It made a happy, laughing sort of a noise.

Drum got the scent of some wild varmint and ran out under the trees with his tail up. He nosed around in the leaves, snuffing hard. He circled, trying to pick up the hottest part of a trail. But Blackie called him in.

"It's likely a ringtail," Blackie said. "You couldn't

catch a ringtail along these here rock bluffs between now and cotton-chopping time next summer. There's too many hollers in these old trees. Too many caves in them rocks."

We rounded a bend in the canyon and saw yellow lamplight through a window. We went up a rocky slope, past a dark hollow place where you could hear water bubbling up out of a spring. We went on up to where the ground leveled off and the high-pitched roof of a rock cabin showed against the skyline.

There was a front gallery to the house. We came to it and the dogs left us and trotted around to the back where the kitchen was. We went up the slab-rock steps. The gallery boards rattled under our feet. The door swung open in front of us, letting out a flood of lamplight. In the lamplight stood the scrawny figure of Grandpa Wilson.

"Howdy, Grandpa!" Blackie shouted.

"Come in this house!" Grandpa shouted back in a high creaky voice.

We walked into a big room with a high ceiling, where a fireplace took up a good part of one wall. The inside of the room was rock, too, painted over white.

"Dave's done told me how you whupped that big boar coon in swimming water," Grandpa cackled.

"Danged if I wouldn't give a purty were I to've seen that fight!"

We propped our gun and ax against the wall and Spud set the lantern down. Blackie took off his hat. Grandpa reached out and got me and Spud by our coat collars and pulled us closer to the fireplace.

"Git over here and back your little bird-sized tail ends up to that fire," he said, cackling like he had a big joke. "I'll bet they're colder'n the butt of a well digger in Alasky!"

They weren't, but it stirred up a good feeling inside me for Grandpa to make such a to-do over just kids like us. We backed up to the fireplace like Grandpa told us. It was red with heat. Grandma Wilson sat beside it, rocking.

Blackie poked his finger through the hole in his pants. He said, "Howdy, Grandma. How you making the winter?"

Grandma looked up at Blackie. Then she reached and took the snuff brush out of her mouth. She forked her fingers over her lips and spat into the fire, making it sizzle. Then she looked back up at Blackie and shook her head.

"Porely, Blackie," she said. "Mighty porely. It'll be the Almighty's mercy if I last to eat a bait of poke greens come spring."

"Why, you look fat and sassy to me, Grandma," Blackie said. "You don't show to be ailin' a-tall!"

Grandma bent her head to shake it, sad-like. "Look at my hair," she told Blackie. "White as a snow bank. Blooming for the grave, I am." She lifted her fat shoulders to take a deep breath, then let it out slowly. "I'm just an old, old woman, boy," she said. "An old, wore-out, man-used woman. Jist a-settin' in this rockin' cheer and blooming for the grave!"

Grandpa came toward us, dragging a couple of cowhide-bottomed chairs. He shoved one toward Blackie and settled his little bony frame in the other. He winked at me and Spud.

Grandpa looked older than Grandma. His face was nothing but bones and wrinkled skin. But his black eyes were bright as a squirrel's and the way his white eyebrows stood wild and shaggy in his face, it gave me the feeling that he was looking any minute for the funniest kind of a joke.

He winked at us again and bared his gums in a grin. Me and Spud grinned and winked back at him.

Grandpa said to Blackie, "That sure must of been some round you boys had with that big boar river coon."

Blackie shoved the chair against the wall and sat on the floor beside it. He put his hat under the chair where it wouldn't get tromped on. "That weren't nothing," he said. "Wait till I tell you about the round we had with Hog Waller just now. That beats the coon fight from a squirrel's jump to the Rocky Mountains."

Grandpa's eyes lit up. "Y'all been mixing it with Hog Waller? Be dog, now! Tell me about it!" Grandpa sat up straight in his chair; he looked as starved out and eager for talk as I get sometimes.

The door to the kitchen opened and Dave Wilson came in; the good smells of woman-cooking followed him in. He said, "Howdy, Blackie!" and came to stand with me and Spud by the fire. He winked at us like Grandpa had, and grinned. I guess he'd learned to wink and grin like that from his grandpa.

"Y'all boys got your appetites whetted up?" he asked.

Grandpa said, "Blackie and the boys is had a round with Hog Waller, Dave. Blackie's fixing to tell about it!"

Dave looked at Blackie and his eyes widened. "The hell you say!" he said.

"Quit cussin' in front of your old granny, Dave!" Grandma said sharply. "It do look like," she complained, "that a pore old soul could go to her grave without the sinful cussin' of her menfolks a-ringing in her ears!"

Dave said, "All right, Granny. It just slipped out."

"Dry up, Ma," Grandpa said. "Blackie's fixing to talk. You catch one of Waller's hogs in a trap, Blackie?"

"Worse'n that," Blackie told him. "Danged old hogs raided our camp and Spud there stuck a foot-long knife in one."

Grandpa jerked up in his chair. "The hell he did!" he hollered, his eyebrows jerking up.

"Pa, quit your cussin'!" Grandma said.

"Goddlemighty, Ma!" Grandpa yelped. "A man's got to talk!"

"There you go again," said Grandma. "Cussin' in front of these here younguns. You ain't satisfied to jist teach your own younguns to cuss; you got to teach it to everybody else's. You got to damn their souls to eternal fire and brimstone!"

Grandma jerked her snuff brush out of her mouth and pointed it at Grandpa. "Fontel Wilson," she said in a voice like the Judgment Day, "you're a wicked old man and may the good Lord condemn you to the fiery pits for the wreck you've made of the fine innocent little girl you tricked into marrying you!"

Grandpa jumped up out of his chair like a mad wasp. He caught the chair by the back and banged it against the floor. "Woman!" he shouted. "Will you simmer down! Confound it, if they aim to bury me before daybreak, I still want to hear about the round these boys had with Hog Waller!"

Grandma's fat shoulders slumped down against the high back of her rocking chair. She ducked her head like she thought Grandpa was fixing to throw the chair at her. She watched Grandpa out of the corners of her eyes and kept quiet.

Dave winked and grinned at Spud and me. Blackie sat and stared at the slits cut in the tops of his hunting shoes. I sat down on the floor beside him.

Grandpa waited till the only sounds we could hear were the snap and crackle of the fire in the chimney and the pan-rattling of Dave's woman Rachael getting supper out in the kitchen. Then he looked at me and Spud.

"Let this be a learning to you boys," he said, speaking mighty grave. "Keep your freedom as long as nature'll permit. Don't never marry till you just can't put it off no longer.

"Now, Blackie," he said, "you go ahead and tell us about that round you boys had with Hog Waller."

"Well—" Blackie said.

But before Blackie could get started, Dave's woman Rachael came to the door and said, "It's ready, Dave!"

That made Dave laugh, and Blackie laughed with him, and Grandpa jumped up out of his chair again and said, "Goddlemighty damn!" and reached and jerked his hat off a wall nail and threw it on the floor and went to stomping it with his feet.

"Pa Wilson!" Rachael scolded. "You quit stomping your Sunday hat and come eat your supper. Now, ain't you ashamed of yourself?"

Dave's woman Rachael looked a lot like her sister Dony, only she was heavier. She seemed quieter, too, and calmer acting.

Grandpa looked up at her and, instead of getting mad like he had with Grandma, he just cracked a grin and bent and picked up his hat and slapped the dust out of it against his leg and hung it back on the wall nail.

"Well, so help me, Rachael!" he grumbled. "I just want to hear Blackie tell about the round him and them boys had with your cousin Ed."

Dave said to us, "Well, if y'all want to eat it all up away from the wife and younguns, come in and have at it."

"Younguns?" said Blackie. "I ain't seen no younguns about this place yet."

Grandpa cackled. "Y' ain't looked clost enough," he said. "It's taken Dave three year, but he's got one in his trap now."

Dave's woman blushed and turned back into the kitchen. Dave grinned, looking proud.

"She's got me wore to a frazzle," he said, "slopping a couple of shoats she's fattening out. Claims she's not going to get caught short on doctor money when her time comes."

Rachael said from the kitchen: "I heard old Doc Cole say once that by rights he owned half the younguns in Mason County. He said they'd never been paid for yet. Nobody's going to say that about my baby!"

"Doctors!" Grandma said scornfully. "A sin and a shame if you ask me. I brung seven younguns into this world and nary a man-doctor was on the place when I done it. In my day, a decent woman had her shame!"

"You coming to supper, Grandma?" Blackie asked.

"I'll set and be waited on," Grandma told him. "I've done my work in this here world. For forty year, I waited on a man and seven boys, hand and foot, worked my fingers to the bone. And when my grandbaby Dave takened a woman, I quit. I set right down in this rocking cheer and told them I was done. I told them from now on till I drawed my last breath, they needn't look for me to turn a hand."

Grandma straightened up and looked proud of herself.

I followed the rest on into the kitchen, wondering what fun a body could get out of just sitting in a rocking chair.

There were brown beans seasoned with fat back on the table, a big bowl of them, and sweet milk and hot cornbread.

"We've run plumb out of table meat," Dave apologized. "I been laying off to go shoot me a fat buck or a big gobbler, but my time's too takened up with horsebreaking. Got after Rachael the other day to let me butcher one them shoats, but Rachael, she hit the ceiling."

Rachael stiffened. "There ain't no doctor going to claim he owns my baby!" she said. She looked straight at Dave to make sure he understood that.

What they had was plenty for me. It was that sweet milk and hot cornbread that I worked on mainly. I hadn't missed it since I'd left home, but now it seemed like I couldn't get enough. I'd drink the top milk off my glass to make room for a batch of cornbread, then crumble it in and take my spoon and go to digging it out again. Cornbread soaked in a glass of milk the right way is sweeter than cake. I put away so much that I knew Mama would have been quarreling at me about my company manners if she'd been there. But she wasn't. And I could tell Rachael didn't mind. She'd just smile at me and Spud and keep dipping in that big crock and filling our glasses as we passed them back.

Watching Dave's woman Rachael pour that milk reminded me of Mama, and all of a sudden I was homesick. I wasn't wanting to quit our hunt and go back, understand, but I just got a big wanting to see Mama and Papa.

Nobody said much; everybody was too busy eating. Rachael waited on us first, then took a big supper to Grandma Wilson. Finally, when the edge of our appetites was worn off, Grandpa said: "Now, I don't want to seem sudden or nothing, Blackie. But when you git around to it, I'd sure like to hear about that run-in you and the boys had with Hog Waller."

Blackie grinned. And this time he got to tell it. He told it from the start, where Spud stuck his throwing knife in the sow, right on up to where Ed Waller ran off, with Snuffy swinging to the seat of his pants. And the way Blackie told it made it better than when it had happened. Or maybe it seemed better because I wasn't scared now. Anyhow, he told it so you were proud of the way Spud had stood up to Ed Waller and proud of how Snuffy had tied into the seat of his pants.

Dave and Grandpa Wilson listened and yelped and hollered with laughing, just like Blackie had done. But Rachael, she looked sober.

"You want to watch Cousin Ed," she warned. "He's not going to see anything funny about what happened. He's going to think it over and get madder and madder. Cousin Ed, he don't like to be laughed at."

"Ed's a blowhard," Dave said. "He don't amount to nothing."

"He's a blowhard, all right, Dave," Rachael said. "But he's got a mean nature, too. I haven't forgot the time people got to laughing about the way Ed's first woman was carrying on with that hog buyer from Uvalde. Next thing anybody knew, that hog buyer was found floating in the Frio River with a hole between his eyes. And Ed had kicked his first woman out." Rachael's eyes got big and dark.

"But woman trouble like that—that's different," Dave said.

"All trouble's the same to Cousin Ed," Rachael said grimly, "any time he's in a fix to get laughed at."

"Speaking of feist dogs," Grandpa broke in, looking straight at me and Spud. "One time I have me a feist. It were a speckled dog. It had more grit than a wad of fish eggs rolled in the sand."

110

He lifted his sweet-milk glass and took another drink, then went on. "I were squirrel hunting, see. Up in the blackjack country. My feist, he trees a squirrel up a big post oak with a mustang grapevine hanging in the top. The leaves is thick; I can't locate this squirrel. D'rectly, I hear a growl. It ain't no squirrel bark, it's a growl. The vines rattle and out of the leaves pokes a varmint nose.

"It were a big boar coon. He's been snoozing up in them shady vines and got woke up by the dog-barking.

"Be dog! Know what he done? Takes one look at my dog and down that tree he comes. Jumps right on my squirrel feist. It's a mortal fact. Jumps right on top of my squirrel feist and tries to eat him alive.

"He soon finds it were a bigger chunk he's bit off than he can swaller, though, this coon does. That feist, he were no bigger than the little end of nothing whittled down to a fine point. But like I say, he were a gritty critter. Ain't no time till he's changed that boar coon's mind about what he wants to eat up. First thing that boar coon knows, he were satisfied and taking to the next closest tree.

"But he weren't shed of that speckled feist. That feist, he has him a back-hold on that boar coon. He's got his teeth clamped tight and his eyes shut. He's set like a turtle; he won't turn loose till it thunders. He's hanging to that coon's back while that coon climbs his tree.

"There were a holler in this second tree, right up under the first fork. The coon, he takes to it, dragging my squirrel feist right in with him. And then you ought to've heered it, the round them two have down in the holler of that tree.

"Me, I set down at the bottom of the tree and listen. I were waiting to see which one would come out of that holler. After about two cigarette smokes, the racket all quiets down, but nothing comes out of the tree. I wait a spell longer, then take my chopping ax and cut the tree down."

Grandpa stopped there to gulp down some more sweet milk. But when he set his glass back on the table, he didn't start talking again. He just looked around like he was waiting for somebody to begin another story.

I couldn't wait any longer. I had to know. "What'd you find, Grandpa?" I asked him.

"Why, nothin'," Grandpa yelped, his bushy white eyebrows jerking up. "Nothin' a-tall, 'cepting a little blood and hair. Y' see, them two had just et each other up!"

Blackie and Grandpa and Dave, they all fell back

112

in their chairs and hollered. I'd sure got sucked in on that one. I felt my neck and ears start burning.

"Now, ain't you menfolks ashamed," Rachael said, "a-picking on a boy like that!" But she was laughing, too.

I wanted to duck down and crawl under the table, I was that hacked. Then Grandpa got up and winked at me and I didn't feel so bad.

"Let's git back to the fire, boy," he said. "I'll spin you one I can prove!"

We went back to the fire where Grandma was still eating. For an old woman with one foot in the grave, Grandma was sure putting away the grub. Grandpa and Dave took chairs. Blackie sat on the floor, and me and Spud sat down on the floor, too, on either side of the warm fireplace. Dave's woman Rachael waited on Grandma till Grandma was finished, then went back into the kitchen to wash the dishes.

Grandpa rolled a little chicken-bill cigarette and lit it. He leaned back in his chair and blew smoke at the ceiling.

"It were 'way back yonder when I'm a shirttail kid," he began. "We're up on the head of Big Devil's River. Me and Buck Teeler, Dobe Whital, and Mexico Jesus. Hunting and fishing; prowling like a kid's got to do. We got us three dogs along.

"One morning we hear the dogs barking treed back up the mouth of a canyon. We grab a gun and tear out to see what the varmint is. It were a paint'er. He were laying up the slant of a stooping tree, jist high enough the dogs have to jump to reach him. And every time a dog jumps, that paint'er slaps him plumb back into yestiddy.

"The paint'er, he sees us boys a-coming. He quits the tree and hits for the roughs. He takes out up a rocky slant toward some bluffs. The dogs, they're making a big racket, but being mighty keerful they don't catch him.

"Dobe takes a running shot at the paint'er, but misses. The paint'er, he growls back at Dobe and makes a high jump for a ledge up the side of the bluff. He lays down and is out of sight.

"How we going to git our paint'er? That's the question. He's right up yonder on that ledge, but the dogs can't git him. And we can't see him. We come up to where the dogs is barking and study the layout. All we can think to do is for three of us to lift the other'n up high enough that he can see to shoot.

"Mexico Jesus, he were the lightest; we choose

him to do the shooting. We give him the gun and start lifting.

"We ain't more'n barely got his head up even with the ledge when there's a fearsome growl above us. Then Mexico Jesus, he screams and lets the gun go off and falls back out of our hands.

"It were enough to clabber a kid's blood, the shape we find Mexico Jesus in when we turn to look. The paint'er, he's reached out and clawed the scalp loose from the back of Mexico Jesus' head and raked it right down over that Mexican kid's face. He's turned it wrong side out, like hulling a possum.

"Now, we're sure in a fix. We're a day's drive from any town. Time we git Mexico Jesus to a doctor, it'll be too late. Mexico Jesus is losing blood fast, and if that scalp ever dries out, it'll shrink and won't cover his head. Something's got to be done now.

"Well, we do it. We shove Mexico Jesus' scalp back over his head and take him back to camp. We got no needle and thread, but what's wrong with a mesquite thorn and horsetail hair? I punch the holes with a mesquite thorn, and Dobe, he pokes the horse hair through and does the tying. Buck Whital, he were the heaviest, he sits on Mexico Jesus and holds him down while we work. Mexico Jesus, he don't have nothin' to do but pitch and holler.

"It were a plumb neat job we do. That Del Rio doctor we take Mexico Jesus to, he swears he couldn't have done better on an operating table. He leaves them stitches like they are, and the scalp heals.

"Mexico Jesus is alive today. Best dadgummed gittar picker in the whole hill country here. Sometimes he plays with Fiddling Tom Waller. Maybe you'll git to hear him someday."

I was shivering all over time Grandpa Wilson finished. I looked at Spud; he was all eyes, too.

"What happened to the panther, Grandpa?" he wanted to know.

Grandpa threw the butt of his cigarette into the fire and started rolling another one. "Now, ain't that jist like a youngun?" he said. "Well, that paint'er, he gits away and we're proud to let him go before he scalps us all. And it were a wonder the big devil don't. Me, I always did hold that the Almighty's got a special angel to look after drunks and damn-fool kids!"

He jerked a thumb toward Grandma and winked. She was asleep. I didn't see how anybody could sleep through a panther tale like Grandpa's, but I guess Grandma'd heard it time and again.

We all sat quiet for a little bit, thinking about Grandpa's panther story. The fire popped and crackled. Then Dave, he recollected the time he found two buck deer with their antlers locked from fighting till they couldn't get loose and had been tied up that way till they were both starved to skin and bones. Dave said he got down off his horse and took a rock and hammered their antlers apart. And then when Dave started for his horse, both buck deer went on the fight and came at him. And Dave's horse got scared and ran off and Dave had to take a tree to keep those fool bucks from hooking and pawing him. After all the trouble he'd gone to to set them free!

And Blackie, he told how one time his dogs bayed something in the top of a blackjack tree that a storm had blown down. And just when he looked in, a big old black sow left her litter of pigs in there and charged him so quick that he couldn't get away. She ran right between his legs and knocked his feet out from under him so he rode her a good long piece, sitting on backwards, before she ran under a tree limb and knocked him off.

Then Grandpa told another one and that made him think of still another. The fire died down. I began to feel drowsy, but I made myself stay awake and listen. Dave's woman Rachael finished with the dishes and came in to listen, too. And then the moon rose and Blackie suddenly came to his feet and said, "Be dog, it's getting late! Me'n the boys aimed to take the dogs for a big round tonight." And much as I liked to coon-hunt, that was one time I didn't want to go. I just wanted to stay and sit by the fire and listen to more talk. Those tales were the best I ever listened to. I couldn't ever remember having a better time in my life!

7

THE moonshine was white magic that night. The rocks and brush and trees all stood out with a hard, shiny blackness. But the light pouring through and around them was soft white stuff, so thick you could almost feel it. It lay in puddles between the brush and rocks. Out on the high flats where cattle like to bed up, the frost-fuzzed tops of old dried cow chips gathered up the light and scattered it, glittering like big crusts of diamonds. Just looking around made me feel like the world was brand spanking new, ready to be lived in for the first time.

We walked through the moonshine, with the dogs working ahead. And walking with me were the tales I'd heard back yonder at Dave Wilson's. Any of these clearings could be the place where Dave found those two buck deer with their antlers locked. When we passed the top of an old dead tree that had blown down, I felt sure it was the one where the wild sow had caught Blackie off guard and run between his legs. And any time I shut my eyes, I could see that big panther reaching over the rim of the ledge to rip Mexico Jesus' scalp loose from his head. I sure did hope I got to see Mexico Jesus sometime.

We jumped a hot coon trail and ran it across a high ridge where the hooked thorns of the catclaw brush clawed the blood out of our legs through our pants. We ran the trail down into a deep shin-oak draw and across another ridge. When the dogs finally barked treed, we found the coon on top of a house-sized boulder that was too high and smooth sided for us or the dogs to climb. We couldn't see the coon on the flat top of the boulder, either, and we stood and wondered awhile how he got up there and how we'd get him down. I said it was sort of like Grandpa's panther story, that maybe we better lift somebody up with a gun; but Blackie had a better idea.

"Why don't we just pitch that Snuffy feist up there," he said. "I'll bet he'll bring that coon down."

So Spud caught Snuffy by the forelegs and I caught him by the hind legs and we gave him a couple of swings back and forth, then whipped him high and let him go.

Snuffy let out a loud yelp as he sailed up through the moonlight. But he hadn't more than hit the top of the rock till we heard him growl. We heard the coon let out a growl, too. Then they tangled and fought over to the edge of the rock where we could see their black figures clawing and biting each other.

Rock and Drum nearly went crazy down there on the ground. They wanted so bad to get up there and help Snuffy with that coon. But they were too heavy for us to throw up; so all they could do was bark and bawl at the tops of their voices and back off and take running jumps at the side of the big rock and claw for holds. They sure did want in on the fight.

We heard Snuffy screeching like he was bad hurt, then he tied into the coon harder than ever. A second later, the big coon came off the top of that rock, snarling and squalling. He hit the ground and Rock and Drum piled into him and it wasn't but a minute till they had him ready for skinning.

But then we couldn't get Snuffy down. Snuffy thought he was up too high for safe jumping. When Spud called to him, all he'd do was whimper and whine and look over the edge of the rock at us and then duck back to keep from falling. It was sort of aggravating, Snuffy being afraid to jump down, after the way he'd climb a high tree trying to get to a coon. But he wouldn't come, and finally all we could do was get a long pole and prop it up beside the rock and let Spud climb up after Snuffy while me and Blackie held the pole.

"Now, dog take it, Spud!" Blackie said. "Don't you git up there and git too scared to come down. I'd have to send Cotton after you. Then he'd likely git scared, too, and I'd have to climb up there after him. First thing you know, there'd be so many on top of that rock that there wouldn't be room for nobody else to come up and git us down."

Spud went to laughing and nearly fell off the pole. But he finally made it and pitched Snuffy to us and climbed back down.

We moved on down the river and the dogs struck another trail, a cold one that warmed up fast. We ran it and ran it, farther and farther down the river, and it got hotter and hotter every minute, but still the hounds didn't tree.

Blackie said he couldn't figure it out. "That old Rock dog was talking possum, I thought, when he started. But now they're working that trail like a coon, only they ain't talking coon. If it was a fox, they'd be moving faster and circling. If it was a bobcat, they'd be making a lot of short fast runs and then losing it ever' time the cat backtracked hisself. It's a puzzler, for certain!"

Blackie pulled at his ducktail, showing how puzzled he was, but he kept urging the dogs on. And finally they treed, 'way out in the middle of a mesquite brush flat.

We hurried out through clumps of shoulder-high sage grass and looked up in the top of a spindly mesquite bush that no varmint with any sense would have climbed. And there it was, a little old scared possum, with his bare tail wound around the tree limb.

"Now, wouldn't that cock your pistol!" Blackie said. "Run a hot trail four mile and all we put up is a possum the size of a corncrib rat. I've heered tell them little old boogers'll run like that, but I never takened any stock in such talk.'·

He caught the little possum by the back of its neck and lifted it down. The possum first growled at us, then played dead. We all looked it over. I held it and felt its little scared heart beating through its soft fur. Then Blackie tried to hang it back up in the tree.

"All he's fit for," he said, "is just to grow up into a possum. We'll leave him to grow a bigger rind."

The possum played so dead that he fell out of the tree and Snuffy grabbed it for a shaking, but Blackie slapped Snuffy loose and picked up the possum and packed him over to a bigger tree and hung him up in a deep fork out of reach of the dogs.

We left him there at the edge of the flat. I looked back once and in the moonlight I could still see that little old possum playing dead in the forks of that mesquite. He hung there, limp as a dishrag.

I guessed that all his life now, that little old possum would think he'd played it smart and fooled us out of killing and skinning him.

Seemed to me it was late enough we ought to be starting back toward camp; but Blackie kept working on down the river. We followed the dogs into a deep bottom where a creek ran head-on into the face of a high cliff and made a horseshoe bend getting out. There were tall pecans and elms growing there and one black shadowed thicket of live-oak saplings. There was a clearing between us and the live-oak thicket, and Rock and Drum padded out into this clearing and suddenly threw up their heads and tails. They'd winded something. They went toward the thicket at a fast trot.

"Now, I wonder what they think they've smelt," Blackie said.

And about that time, we heard a sharp *put-put-puttreet!* come out of the live oaks and then the whole top of the thicket blew up, and big dark shapes thundered up into the air and shot off through the moonlight in every direction.

Blackie jumped worse than me and Spud. "Lordy mercy!" he yelped, "I wish them old gobblers wouldn't do that. They just scare the cold whey out of me!"

The wild gobblers hit the ground out away from us a couple of hundred yards. We heard the thrash of their wings in the brush and the rattle of rocks as they took to the hills. Then we heard the booming voice of old Drum open and wheeled to look. Yonder over a little bald rise raced old Drum with his nose not three feet from the tail feathers of a big gobbler. The gobbler ran with his neck stretched out and his big wings about half spread, and he was sure toeing it. Drum was crowding him for all he was worth; and here came Rock, lifting his high-pitched voice in wild yelps, and back behind him apiece was the black feist Snuffy, just a-screeching.

Blackie said, "Come on, we'll git that old gobbler!" and left out in a long-stepping run. I took out after him, and Spud followed me. We had us a wild gobbler chase going!

It sure was a fast one. Crowded like Drum was crowding him, that old gobbler didn't run more than a quarter of a mile till he quit the ground. I heard the booming thunder of his wings as he whipped himself into the air and thought the race was all over. But Blackie said no. He said a gobbler wouldn't hardly change his course of flight after he'd left the ground. Blackie said old Drum knew which direction that gobbler was going and would keep knocking right along, as near under him as he could stay, and be ready to pick up his trail again the minute he hit the ground.

And that's how it was. Drum ran silent for a good long ways, then opened again, still headed in the same direction—downriver. And in just a little bit, old Rock opened right up beside him.

The sound of their voices running that gobbler

was different from when they ran a coon. Wilder and a lot more eager. It pulled at me harder, and there for a little bit I was even outrunning Blackie.

Spud got behind, of course, and got to complaining that he couldn't keep up. But me and Blackie didn't pay any attention to Spud. He couldn't keep up with us; but you could bet your bottom dollar he'd never let us get more than a fifty-yard lead on him.

The gobbler flew once more, but it was a short flight this time, and Blackie said that'd be the last one. Blackie said a big old fat gobbler never could make more than a couple or three flights altogether like that till he'd call it quits. He said it wouldn't be no time now till the hounds put him up a tree.

Blackie was right again. We heard the hounds pick up the gobbler's trail and run it just a little piece. Then we heard them tree.

We nearly had our tongues hanging out when we trotted up to the elm tree the dogs were baying under. We hadn't run so far, but we'd sure been running fast.

It was a low scrubby elm the gobbler had taken to. He was down on the lowest branches where a man could reach him with a stick. He sat there with his wings bracing him against the branches. We could skylight him and see that his beak was hung open and he was panting from his run. He'd shut his beak and say *put-tut-teet!* and crane his long neck down out of the tree limbs to look at us and then lift his head and go back to panting again. Sometimes we could even see his tongue working back and forth, he was panting so hard.

The hounds jumped up and down, barking at him, and Snuffy tried to climb the elm but the trunk was too straight-up and smooth.

Blackie told us to get us some clubs and get set before the old gobbler rested up and left out on us. "We could shoot him," Blackie said, "but you can't hardly kill a wild gobbler with a .22 hull. You just cripple him so he'll die later. A wild gobbler, he can dang nigh pack off as much lead as a buck deer!"

We searched around and got us some short lengths of dead tree branches for clubs. Then Blackie went up under the turkey and set himself and drew back his club and took aim at the gobbler's neck and cut down on him.

The stick struck the gobbler's head and out he came, big wings flopping. The dogs ran to grab him and we ran in to beat off the dogs and just then Blackie yelled, "Hand him another! He ain't dead yet!"

I wheeled, and sure enough, there the old gobbler was, coming to his feet, tall as I was. His beak was right up in my face and before I even thought, I reached out and grabbed him by the neck.

That really brought him to life. He climbed right up in my face. He swarmed all over me, flogging me with his wing butts, clawing at my neck and stomach with his big toenails.

"Lordy mercy, hang with him, Cotton!" I heard Blackie yell.

A baying hound lunged in, knocking me down. I fell flat of my back, smothered with feathers and blinded by wing blows. But I kept my hold on that neck and hit the ground rolling and came up on my knees with the gobbler pinned between them.

I got my other hand on that long, loose-hided neck and gave it a hard wrench and felt the bones snap between my hands. The big gobbler stiffened all over; warm blood gushed out of his mouth and spattered in my face. And for a second there, I felt the wild savage, half-sickening thrill of having killed a live thing with my own bare hands!

Blackie held up the big gobbler by his broken neck and admired him in the moonlight.

"Now, won't that make a potful of fancy eating?" he exclaimed. He stuck his finger in that hole in his pants and twisted it around while he looked off up at one bunch of stars and then another. Then he added: "I bet it would sure pleasure Fiddling Tom Waller and his womenfolks to take them this old bird. I bet they ain't set tooth in a fat wild gobbler like this in no telling how long."

All the fun and excitement of the hunt started draining out of me, leaving me tired and cold and recollecting that queer look in Blackie's eyes when he'd stared at Dony Waller the other afternoon. And it came to me, too, that all night we'd been coming straight down the river instead of hunting in a circle so we'd be close to camp when it was over. I hated to get suspicious of Blackie, but it sure looked now like he'd had it in mind all along to head straight for Fiddling Tom Waller's place.

I guess maybe Spud had the same uneasy feeling. Spud said: "Why don't we take it back and let Dave Wilson's woman cook it? She fed us supper and Dave claimed they was short of meat."

Blackie looked at Spud and then back at the stars again. "We're all too wore out to make that long haul back to camp tonight," he said. "It ain't but two-three mile down to Fiddling Tom's place. We'll bed up for a sleep there and hunt back tomorrow night."

He slung the gobbler across his shoulder. "That's the thing to do," he said. "We'll let Fiddling Tom's womenfolks give this gobbler a baking while we catch up on our rest. When it comes to fixing up turkey-and-dressing, you can't beat woman-cooking.

He struck out down the river and me and Spud followed. The moonshine glinted on the big gobbler's back feathers. It lay in the cow trail ahead of us, as soft and thick and white as ever. But a lot of the magic was gone out of everything. Somehow, I couldn't help feeling like Blackie was cheating on us.

8

THE sun was just ready to come up when we breasted through the thick tangle of bee brush in Fiddling Tom Waller's calf pasture. We climbed over the rock fence beside his cow lot. There were three milk cows in the lot; they saw us and got up stiffly, rattling their hoofs and snapping their joints. They grunted and belched and stretched the sleep out of their muscles.

We rounded the corn crib and headed down the trail toward the cabin. It was a squatty log cabin that sat back in a grove of blackjack oaks. It fitted in under those blackjacks so well, you had the feeling it had grown up there with the trees. The blue-white smoke of a fresh-built fire poured out of the slab-rock chimney. The smoke curled and twisted up through the bare trees, then spread and hung out over them like a giant umbrella.

The front door of the cabin opened before we got there. Fiddling Tom Waller, tall, white headed and bony, came outside in his sleeping drawers. He walked across the gallery in his bare feet and then on out across the sandy yard. He stopped and leaned against the picket-pole fence, gazing off down the river canyon.

I guessed Fiddling Tom's woman did him like Mama did me. She wouldn't let me stand on the gallery and wet off the edge in ordinary weather. It had to be sleeting or snowing; that's the only way Mama would put up with it.

Fiddling Tom didn't see us coming till Blackie hollered at him. It didn't make Fiddling Tom jump and act guilty like I'd of done, caught that way. He just turned his head and looked at us, then went back to staring off down the river canyon.

He waited till we came through the yard gate, then

pointed a long bony finger at the sun rising up out of a big pool of water a mile downriver. "Look at that," he said, "if you want to see the hand of the Almighty in all its glory. Look at the light on that there water. Look at the color of them there hills. There ain't no picture-painting artist ever got them colors put down right. There ain't none never will!"

Fiddling Tom's drawers were skimpy in the legs and sleeves, baggy in the seat. His gray hair was sleep rumpled. There was a week's growth of beard on his face. But while he stood there in the early-morning light, so tall and grave, you forgot those things. You just saw the gentle, worshiping look in his eyes as he stared at the glory of that sunrise. You just saw the fineness and goodness in his long face. You thought of that Sunday-school card picture of Jesus Christ where he's standing on the mountain top and looking out on a world he's feeling sorry for.

The hounds trotted in out of the brush, making for the kitchen. Dony, she came to the door.

"Papa," she scolded. "You come in this house and put on some clothes. Come a day you'll catch your death, standing out there in your drawers."

Fiddling Tom stood a little longer, like he hated to leave; then he turned and went into the house.

Dony patted his shoulder when he went past her.

Then she looked at me and at Spud and at the big gobbler I was packing now. Finally, like she was saving the best for the last, she looked at Blackie! She looked straight at him, her eyes beginning to sparkle while her lips parted in a pleased, secret half-smile. She didn't say anything.

Blackie said: "We got off down this way and these little old younguns, they was all tuckered out. I figured maybe to rest 'em up here and hunt back tonight!"

Dony's eyebrows lifted. "You sure don't let any grass grow under your feet," she said. She measured him with a long look and asked: "You think you're on the trail of something?"

Blackie stiffened. That same queer, bright shine was in his eyes again.

"You mighty right, I'm on the trail of something," he said.

Dony threw back her head and laughed. "I like a man who don't let the grass grow under his feet," she said. Then she laughed again, a kicking-up-your-heels sort of laugh that made you want to laugh with her.

But I didn't know what there was to laugh about. Like day before yesterday, their talk didn't make sense. It was the kind of talk grown people use to make a kid feel left out.

A coal-black hound-pup with a stub tail and long droopy ears came out from under the gallery steps. He didn't come out barking and twisting and wringing his tail like most pups would have done. He just walked out, slow, like he wasn't much interested, and came over to me and sniffed the dead gobbler. When he finished sniffing it, he stood and looked up at me with sad, lonesome eyes.

"Be dog!" said Blackie. "Now, that there's sure a fine-looking pup. Ain't seen a crow-black hound like that since that bar' hog kilt that old Nigger dog of Cotton's daddy's!"

"Mexico Jesus gave him to me," Dony said. "Somebody gave him to Mexico Jesus and Mexico Jesus, he couldn't do anything with him, so he gave him to me. But I can't do anything with him either. He won't trail. He won't catch. I can't even make him mind."

Blackie said: "Could be you don't know how to manage a hound-pup."

"He won't take up with me," Dony said. "He won't take up with nobody. He just eats what I feed him and lays around under the house with an old wild housecat that's denning under there. He won't give me a chance to handle him."

Blackie snapped his fingers at the black pup and made a kissing sound with his lips. "Come here, pup," he said.

The black pup turned his head and looked at Blackie. But he wouldn't go to nim; he wouldn't even wag his stub tail. He just looked at Blackie and swung his head back and started staring at me again.

"Well, now, he's a quare one, all right," Blackie said. He looked down at the pup, studying him. "You ever put him with grown dogs?"

"Papa tried," Dony said. "He took him out with the Dobbs boys' hounds one night. Waited till they struck a trail and then turned him loose. All he did was come on back home. If I could find somebody he'd take up with, I'd give him away!"

Fiddling Tom came to the door. He had his shoes on now. "That there's a one-man dog," Fiddling Tom said, "but he ain't found the right man yet. He won't never be no account till he finds the right man to take up with."

"I've heered tell of dogs like that," Blackie said.

Spud said: "Papa had one once. Wouldn't mind nobody but him. Wouldn't pay attention to nobody but him. Wouldn't do a thing for nobody else."

"That's right," Fiddling Tom said. "Knowed one once when I'm a shirttail kid. Could have combed Texas and half of the Injun Territory and not found a better dog. Had a voice purty as an army bugle. But one man was all he'd do for!"

I never had heard an army bugle blow, but the way Fiddling Tom talked you knew it sure had to sound pretty. Moving cautious so as not to scare him away, I poked my fingers out to the black pup. Just as cautious, he lifted his nose and smelled them. He didn't lick them or wag his tail or anything. He just smelled them and then stood back and looked at me again.

From inside the house, Fiddling Tom's woman called Dony. And Dony said, "Yes, Mama," and shook her head so that her long hair sparkled in the sunlight. She looked at Blackie with her eyebrows lifted again and went back into the house.

Fiddling Tom said for us to come in, too, and that the womenfolks would soon have it on the table. Blackie said he didn't want to put them out none and Fiddling Tom said it wouldn't put them out none a-tall, so we all went in.

Just before I stepped through the door, though, I looked back and saw that the black hound-pup had followed us across the yard. He was still watching me, too, and now there was a sort of begging look in his eyes. For a minute, I had the feeling that if I'd go back, he'd maybe wag his stub tail at me.

But Fiddling Tom was pulling the door to, shutting out the morning cold; so I went on in and left the pup standing there in the yard.

Inside the room there was a big bed with posts so tall they reached nearly to the ceiling. It sat in one corner of the room, close to the fireplace, and it had a pretty red and yellow and green Mexican blanket on it. Up on the wall at the head of the bed was a board shelf with a fiddle case on it. And above the fireplace on the mantel was an eight-day clock and above that a deer-horn rack holding a long, square-barreled Winchester. On the walls of the room hung a picture of the Alamo, like the one at home that I'd peddled salve to get, and one of Jesus nailed to the cross and bleeding from the crown of thorns, and a big plaster of Paris plaque with red letters spelling out GOD BLESS OUR HAPPY HOME.

It was a good comfortable lived-in kind of a room, with plenty of cowhide-bottomed chairs to sit in.

Fiddling Tom sat down on the edge of the bed and motioned us to take chairs, and Spud did, but Blackie squatted down beside one. I just stood holding the big gobbler by the neck and wondering what to do with it.

Fiddling Tom's woman came to the door with

biscuit flour on her hands, wiping it off on her apron. She was a little bit of a thing, with the quick eye and fast step of a woman able to run down and catch her own frying chickens. She wore her hair skinned up from her face and balled into a tight knot on top of her head, but it didn't make her look ugly like it does a lot of women. It just made her look like a little old prissy girl trying to act dignified and important.

She said: "It do beat all, Blackie Scantling, how far you can smell a woman's cooking!"

Blackie grinned. "Now, don't you go trying to pick no fuss with me, Miz Waller," he said. "I'm paying my keep with that fat gobbler I brung."

I slipped the gobbler off my back and held it around so Fiddling Tom's woman could see it.

"Land of Moses!" she said, her eyes widening. "Now, ain't that a dandy!" She lifted her voice. "Dony!" she called, "come look at this fat gobbler Blackie brung."

Dony said from the kitchen, "I seen it, Mama," but she came and stood in the door anyway, where she could look at Blackie.

Blackie said: "Jumped a bunch out of a roost up in that Devil's Den holler. Old dogs takened this'n for a heat and treed him. I knocked him out with a

140

stick, but Cotton here, he's the one that got the meat. Wrassled him down with his bare hands. Waltzed him all over an acre of ground. Had a-been there was fiddle music and a caller, you couldn't a-told him and that gobbler from square-dance partners."

Blackie was making a real big something out of my killing that wild gobbler. It was sure nice to be the center of notice like that, but it hacked me, too, and I could feel the red crawling up from my neck into my face.

"Well, it do beat all," Fiddling Tom's woman said. She reached for the gobbler and said, "But how come a smart woman like Cora Kinney letting her onliest boy run footloose in the woods after Blackie Scantling? I can't make that out. Anything could happen to him. Anything on earth."

Fiddling Tom stood up. He reached down his fiddle case and said solemnly: "There's a time when a boy can lay his belly on the ground and feel the heartbeats of the earth coming up to him through the grass roots. That's his time to prowl. That's his time to smell the par-fume of the wild flowers, to hear the wind singing wild in his ears, to hurt with the want of knowing what's on the yonder side of the next ridge. The Almighty, he never meant for a boy to miss them things when that time comes!"

Fiddling Tom had his fiddle out of the case by this time and was picking little pretty sounds out of the strings with his big thumb.

His woman looked at him with Dony's half-smile on her lips. "Yes," she said, "and the Almighty never meant for a man to fiddle in his drawers before he's ever et a bite of breakfast. Now, you git them clothes on, Tom."

Fiddling Tom looked at his woman, then back down at his fiddle. "I got a new one that sure ought to be played," he said.

You could look at the face of Fiddling Tom's woman and know she was going to give in before she said: "Well, if it just can't wait. But you make it short, now. Them biscuits is nearly done!"

Still standing, Fiddling Tom tightened his bow and tucked his fiddle under his chin. He stood like that for a second, his bow held in his left hand while he looked out through the window at the sun coming up down the canyon. I knew he'd forgotten us already. A sad, faraway look came into his eyes. He reached over with his bow and touched a high note as bright and sharp edged as a new knife. You could feel it cutting right through you, quick and clean. Then his long bony fingers ran down the neck of the fiddle and he brought his bow back over and down to the

coarse strings to where the music was low and lonesome.

I'd heard fiddle music, but I'd never known it
could stab you like a thorn and make you like the
sting of it. I'd never heard none that made you want
to laugh and cry at the same time. Or made you see
the sun coming up out of a big pool of water, while
the frogs hollered from the wild onions growing
along the banks and the speckled bass popped their
tails in the shoal water and the mockingbirds sat in
the tops of the cedars and sang like they do at daybreak.

That music, it filled the house till the rafters were
humming. It filled the house and seeped out through
the cracks between the logs and rode the smoke out
up the chimney. And even outside, it whimpered
and called and cried.

The hounds waiting at the kitchen door—they
couldn't stand it. They started crying, and up
through the floor boards came the whimpering howl
of the black pup, sad and mournful. The hurt of
the music put tears to stinging my eyes till I wanted
to get Fiddling Tom to stop, but was ashamed to let
on how I felt. Then, just in time, Fiddling Tom cut
it off, high noted and quick, like he'd started it,
leaving me feeling clean washed and wrung out.

When the hounds quit howling, Fiddling Tom's woman said lightly, "Well, if fiddling will get the sun up, that ought to have it!" But I noticed she'd had to gulp hard before she could talk and I guessed I wasn't the only one who wanted to cry. Then she said, "Oh, land of Moses, my biscuits!" and rushed off to see about them.

From the kitchen she called out, "Git them clothes on, Tom!"

Dony stood there in the door and bit on her underlip and watched Blackie. And Blackie stared down at his shoes with a funny look on his face. Fiddling Tom went to putting his fiddle back in its case, handling it as loving and gentle as a woman putting a new baby to bed.

Blackie looked up, pulling at his ducktail. "That's quare music," he said, shaking his head. "It's good listening, but a man'd sure have him a go of it trying to swing-dance to that tune."

"That wasn't a swing-dance tune," Dony explained proudly. "That wasn't no tune you ever heard played before. That wasn't no tune Papa ever played before. Papa made that one up while he was out there looking at the sun coming up. Them tunes just come to him. He can watch the sun go down or listen to a storm a-brewing or maybe just be looking at the

black chunks of shadows the trees make in the moonlight, and a fine tune like that will come to him and
he can play it. I don't guess there ever was a fiddling
man like Papa."

Dony was proud of her papa's fiddling; she was
trying to help Blackie understand it.

Fiddling Tom said: "Come dark tonight, and
maybe so we'll have some swing-dance tunes. Mexico
Jesus, he's herding sheep back over on Salt Branch.
Lots of times of a night, he brings his git-tar up
and we set and have a go of it together. There's a
heap of good music in Mexico Jesus."

Fiddling Tom lifted his shirt and pants down off
the bedpost and pulled them on and his woman
called us in to eat and we all went into the kitchen,
with Fiddling Tom buttoning up as he went.

There were hot biscuits and cornmeal mush and
butter and fried middling meat and wild honey with
a catclaw flavor, with plenty of milk to wash it all
down. Fiddling Tom's womenfolks, they sure did
set a good table.

But it was warm there in the kitchen and I was
so worn out from the night's hunt that I didn't get
to eat more than four or five biscuits before things
got to swinging around in front of me and I couldn't
keep my eyes propped open. And I guess Spud was

in the same fix, because pretty soon, Fiddling Tom's woman said: "Why, look at the poor little wretches. Too sleepy to bite a biscuit. Dony, go fix a bed for these little old younguns and put 'em in it. I declare, it do beat all how boys and menfolk will kill theirselves a-hunting."

Dony laughed and got up and came around the table. "Bless their little old hearts," she said. "When I marry, I'm going to have fourteen just like 'em."

She led us to bed in a shed room on the back of the house and threw back the quilts and said, "Pile in." And we piled in and she took our shoes off for us and pulled the cover up and kissed us both before she left.

The last thing I recollect was hoping that Mexico Jesus would come that night. I sure did want to see a man that a panther had scalped.

9

LATE sunlight sneaked in under the low eaves of the west room and roused me. For a minute, I couldn't recollect where I was. I rubbed my eyes and caught a slight movement out in the middle of the floor. It was Dony's black hound-pup, standing there with his head cocked to one side, studying me. I stuck out my hand and made a low kissing sound.

The pup came and sniffed of my hand again. Carefully, he licked out a warm wet tongue and ran it over my fingers.

He backed off quick, then, but it was enough. He'd licked my hand! He never had licked the hand of anybody else, but he'd licked mine!

The warmth of his smooth wet tongue ran up my arm and spread all over me. I sat up in bed, stirred with the wonder of it.

Spud woke up and rubbed his eyes. "Huh? What is it?" he asked.

"The pup!" I told him. "He licked my fingers!"

The sleep went out of Spud's eyes. "He did?" he said. "Lemme see!"

He sat up and bent over in bed so he could look past me. But the pup wouldn't lick my fingers now. Not with Spud watching. I made the kissing sound again and said, "Come here, pup!" He looked like he'd like to and once he wagged his stub tail a little. But he wouldn't come up and lick my hand again. And when I slid out from under the covers to go to him, he turned and padded out the door into the yard.

Good cooking smells came from the kitchen where we could hear Fiddling Tom's woman puttering around. We put on our shoes, Spud and I did, and went out on the back gallery to wash up—just in case she was to call us in to eat or something.

I was disappointed about the pup; I wished he wasn't so shy. But he'd licked my hand; that was something.

Fiddling Tom's woman stuck her head out the kitchen door and smiled at us. "That gobbler ain't quite done yet," she said. "Y'all can go out front and help that man of mine put the sun to bed. Or see what's keeping Dony and Blackie so long at the cow lot. I dee-clare, them two could have milked and stripped a dozen cows by now."

We dried our faces and went through the fire-place room and out on the front gallery, pleased to know what was expected of us. A lot of times, women-folks will just let strange kids stand around under-foot and be uncomfortable, not knowing what else to do.

We found Fiddling Tom sitting with his chair propped against the cabin wall, studying the sunset with a rapt expression on his long face. He turned and gave us a brief stare before swinging his gaze back to the banners of red and orange light flaring from behind a purple cloud. He said nothing and we knew that he hadn't really seen us, that he was off in some pretty dream world. We went down the steps and out the gate and headed for the cow lot.

We stopped at the corner of the corncrib, though —then stepped back quick, uneasy and somehow a little ashamed at what we'd seen. That is, I was. Spud stuck a tongue in his cheek and looked wise.

It was Blackie, with Dony hemmed up in the corner of the cow lot. He was handing her a lot of sweet-talk in a low urgent voice. He held her close and was running one hand up and down her back.

We stood for a moment, peeping between the interlocking butts of the crib logs.

Dony wasn't trying to fight Blackie off. She had her hands on his shoulders and her face was all pinked up. Her breath was coming quick, and her eyes were bright, looking into his. But she was laughing at him, shaking her head.

"Now, listen, hound-dog man," she scolded. "You've hit a cold trail. I won't listen to no kind of talk like that!"

Blackie looked surprised. "You mean," he said, "you ain't interested?"

Dony's face got sober. Suddenly, she ducked her head and leaned it against his shoulder, breathing hard. "Oh, Blackie!" she said.

Then she stiffened and pushed him away. "You heard me," she said. "When I listen to that kind of talk, I'll be holding the marrying papers in my hand!"

She stood and looked up at him, her eyes big and hoping. She almost quit breathing, seemed like, waiting for Blackie to say what she wanted to hear.

But Blackie wouldn't say it. He backed off, shaking his head. "Well—I'll—just—be—tee-total—damned!" he said. He looked her up and down and shook his head again. He took a deep breath and let it out slow.

"Chickabiddy," he said, grinning, "you sure got a fancy bait laid out, but this old fox has robbed too many pretty sets to stick his foot in a trap now!"

He slapped his leg and laughed, trying to make a joke of it.

Dony swallowed hard. "Well," she said quietly, "in that case, I guess we just as well take this milk on up to the house and eat supper."

She turned to lift the full buckets of milk off the wire hooks hanging from a mesquite limb. Me and Spud whirled and skinned out for the house. We didn't want to get caught listening in where we weren't wanted.

We sat on the front gallery steps and kept quiet so we wouldn't disturb Fiddling Tom. We watched with him while the banners of light faded to pink, then grew purple, and finally disappeared altogether, leaving the chill dusk to set in.

We heard Dony come in the back way and ask her mama where to find the milk strainer. We heard Dony's mama giving her down the country about something or other, talking too low for us to understand. Then their voices lifted, carrying to us, sharp and clear.

"Now, I'm telling you, Dony," Fiddling Tom's woman said. "You better fight shy of that Blackie Scantling. That hound-dog man, he ain't the marrying kind."

"Any man's the marrying kind," Dony said flatly, "if the right woman gets after him."

I straightened up in alarm, listening closer.

Dony's mama said: "I don't see what you want with him. I'll allow he's cute as a bug, with that slick tongue of his and that little ducktail of hair curling up behind. But land of Moses, child, you'd never on this green earth hold him. No woman can hold him. He's a prowler!"

"I can hold him," Dony said. "I can prowl with him; that'll hold him!"

"And who'd make the living, I'd like to know? Not a trifling no-account man like Blackie!"

Dony laughed. "You're a fine one to ask that. You, living all your life with a left-handed fiddler, then trying to tell me about a trifling, no-account man!"

"Dony!" Her mama's voice was sharp. "You can't talk to me like that about your papa. There never was a better-hearted man born."

"You don't have to tell me that, either," Dony said. "I know what a saint my papa is. He just barely plays second fiddle to God Almighty. It'll crowd me ever to love another man like I love Papa."

"Then you hush up about him."

Dony went on like she hadn't heard: "But loving him don't blind me to how he sets and fiddles and leaves the heavy work to his womenfolks!"

I wished they wouldn't say things like that. It didn't seem right, with Fiddling Tom out there listening—if he was hearing a word. He didn't look like he was listening. He was staring at that hog-back ridge the sun had sunk behind, and from the look on his face, he might still be lost in that pretty dream.

I swapped glances with Spud. Spud winked and grinned. I guess Spud was used to a lot of family rowing. I guess this wasn't making him uneasy like it was me. He got up and stretched and walked out

across the yard and picked up a broken hoe handle
and started jabbing it into the ground.

Inside the house, Fiddling Tom's woman pleaded:
"But, honey, he'll neg-glect you. He'll break your
heart a thousand times!"

"Sure," said Dony. "Just like Papa breaks yours.
And mend it the same way. When he gets around to
it. A little sweet-talk and a spank on the bottom.
That's enough, when you've got the right man."

"Dony!" Fiddling Tom's woman was shocked.
"Where'd you ever learn about things like that!"

Dony laughed again. "From you, Mama—and
from Papa," she said. "I've seen that fiddling man
work and fret you to a frazzle. I've seen him neg-
lect you till you didn't want to live another day.
And then I've watched him set you right back up in
heaven with one little pinch. Just one pinch, and
your heart was up in your eyes and your knees got
wobbly and you were done his again, right then—
ready for the taking!"

Her mama gasped. "Well, it do beat all," she said,
half laughing, "how a body's younguns'll catch on!"

"I've caught on a-plenty," Dony bragged. "I've
learnt how wasted I'd feel on some old money-grub-
bing kind of a man. Hog Waller's that kind. I got to
have something special. One way or another, I'll get

him, too. And when I do, I'll know how to hold him. Don't you worry none about that!"

I sat there on the front gallery steps and tried to tell myself that Blackie was too smart for Dony to trap; but I wasn't right sure now that he was. It sounded like Dony had her mind made up, and I'd heard Papa say, time and again, that when a woman sets her mind to a thing, a man might as well knuckle under; come hell or high water, she'll get her way.

I didn't want Dony to get her way. It wasn't that I didn't like Dony. I liked her fine. She was pretty to look at, and she had a laugh that set your insides to singing. Why, down yonder at the cow lot when Blackie was crowding her so close, I'd even felt sorry for her. But I didn't want her marrying Blackie. Blackie ought to be free to prowl with me. I didn't want him tied hand and foot like Papa.

Dony's black pup came out from under the house to wag a stump tail and shyly lick my hand again. But Blackie strolled in from the cow lot just then, and the pup wouldn't stay.

Blackie had an ear of corn in his hand. He was picking grains loose from the cob and thumping them into the air and catching them in his mouth, then cracking them between his teeth. He caught sight of a couple of doves that came winging low, whistling plaintive and shooting through the air like bullets. He thumped a grain high overhead, into the path of the doves, and gave a short laugh when the doves swerved from their course to dodge it.

Dony came to the door behind us and said, "Y'all can get washed up for supper now, Papa." She went on out toward the woodpile, and Blackie winked at her as she went past; but Dony made like she didn't see him. She picked up the ax and went to cutting wood for the fireplace.

Fiddling Tom sighed and got up and said, "You boys want to come wash up a little?" And Blackie guessed it'd be worth a washing to get to eat some of that woman-cooked gobbler, and followed Fiddling Tom through the house to the wash pan. Me'n Spud, we went with them and washed again. It might have looked like we had bad manners and were too anxious for supper to have said we'd already washed.

Fiddling Tom's woman was just putting the big gobbler on the table when we went in to sit down. I never saw a prettier sight than that old bird made, lying flat of his back in the platter, with both drumsticks in the air. He was browned to a turn and banked with cornbread-and-wild-onion dressing. The smell set my mouth to watering.

156

Blackie slipped in behind the table and sat on a long bench against the kitchen wall. His eyes feasted on the gobbler and he allowed to Fiddling Tom that a man was sure in luck to have womenfolks who could do that fancy a job of gobbler baking.

That made Fiddling Tom sit up and look proud. It ought to have pleased his woman, too, seemed like. But the tight set to her pretty mouth didn't ease off a bit. She just turned and went back into the kitchen for a jar of wild plum jelly.

That morning at daylight, Fiddling Tom's woman had been glad to see us and hooraw with Blackie. But now, best I could tell, she was like Mama—put out with him.

Fiddling Tom drew a butcher knife on the gobbler and went to slicing off big white slabs of breast. He forked the meat onto our plates and scooped us out plenty of dressing. He poured brown gravy over the dressing and said to fall to and help ourselves. We didn't have to be urged to start putting it away.

We heard Dony throw down an armload of wood at the fireplace. She came into the room and Blackie told her she better come dive in, that it was going fast. Dony didn't answer; she just smiled at me and Spud and went to helping her mama wait on the table.

It sure made it handy for good fast eating, having a couple of women stand back and wait on us. We didn't hardly have to reach for a thing. The minute our plates ran low, Dony or her mama was right there, stacking on more potatoes and gravy or turkey. I wished Mama would do that way at home all the time instead of just when we had company.

The bones piled up beside Blackie's plate. He turned and lifted the window sash behind him. He propped it with a stick, then pitched the bones outside.

"That way," he said, laughing, "there ain't nobody can count the pieces I've et."

He broke off his laugh to lean farther out the window, peering down at the ground. He pulled his head back inside and said to Dony: "Is this that old wild tomcat of your'n?"

Dony came around and crawled in on the bench beside Blackie. She looked out the window.

"That's him," she said. "Been laying up under the house for three-four weeks now. Trying to take up with us for the winter."

"Borned in the woods, I'll bound," Blackie allowed. "Wilder'n a wolf!"

"Too wild to eat at first," Dony said. "But I been dropping him pieces of bread and gentling him down." She looked straight at Blackie and added: "I got a gift for taming wild things!"

But if that meant anything special, Blackie didn't notice. "Now, ain't he smacking them turkey bones?" he said.

"I guess so!" Dony said. "That's the first time he's had a bait of anything here besides cold cornbread. You'd do some smacking over turkey, too, if cold cornbread was all you ever got to eat."

Blackie laughed at that and Dony laughed with him. They both had their heads right together, looking out of the window. Dony turned to look at Blackie. In the yellow lamplight, I could see her eyes lit up and dancing again, like they hadn't been since she'd come from the cow lot. The warm color was crawling back up into her cheeks, too. Dony was sure a pretty thing when her eyes were all lit up and dancing that way. It made me sort of glad to see her acting happy again.

But it didn't look like Fiddling Tom's woman was glad. There wasn't any warm, happy light shining in her eyes. She spoke sharp to Dony, telling her to go bring her papa a hot biscuit.

Fiddling Tom's woman was right handy to the kitchen door, herself, but she made Dony get up and go get the biscuit.

I picked up a drumstick to gnaw on and got up to go see the tomcat. Spud got up, too, and came in from the other side of Blackie. Night was right at hand now, but the window sill was low to the ground, so that we could see the head and shoulders of a big black-and-white-spotted tomcat reaching out from under the floor for another turkey bone. He cut a cautious eye up at us and sneaked back out of sight to do his eating.

"Don't you know that old wild scogie would have wall-eyed fits," Blackie speculated, "if a man was to reach down and grab hold of him! Bet he'd shuck that hide, trying to git a-loose!"

Behind him Fiddling Tom chuckled and Dony came in, bringing him his hot biscuit, and said: "Well, I sure don't want to be the one doing the grabbing. Wild as that old thing is, he'd eat you up alive."

Blackie snorted. "Why, I wouldn't be afraid to grab him. I've had my hands on a lot of wild critters in my time and never got clawed up."

"Most of them wild critters wasn't trying much to get away," Dony said, with an edge to her voice. "Go on and grab him. See how your luck holds out!"

Blackie threw Dony a look over his shoulder and sucked in a quick breath.

"Pitch that drumstick down there, Cotton, and

toll him out," Blackie said. "I can handle him!"

I took a last bite off my drumstick and dropped it down on the ground. The tomcat eased out to get it and Blackie reached down and snatched him up. Blackie always did have a quick hand.

The cat squalled bloody murder, just like Blackie had figured. But he twisted out of Blackie's grip and balled up on his hand, scratching and clawing. I guess Blackie hadn't figured on that.

Blackie yelled. He fell back into the room, bumping his head on the window sash, trying to shake the tomcat loose. But the tomcat was scared, and he fought back with all he had. He climbed right up Blackie's arm, spitting and snarling, his hair standing on end. He slapped Blackie in the face, then jumped as far as he could.

He landed on the table and kicked turkey and dressing to the ceiling. He skidded in the gravy dish, leaped for the kitchen door; but Fiddling Tom's woman was there. She screamed and then Dony screamed. The cat spun around and tore into the fireplace room.

Blackie stood up, clutching a bleeding hand and saying, "Goddlemighty damn!" Fiddling Tom just sat there at the table with a startled look in his eyes, waving a forkful of turkey breast in the air.

Inside the fireplace room the tomcat went crazy.

The doors and windows were shut; he knew he was trapped and he was frantic to get out. He circled the room, squalling and spitting. He knocked over chairs. He leaped up and tried to climb the walls and fell back to the floor. He rattled the window-panes, trying to jump through. We could hear things clattering to the floor.

It was Dony who let him out. Seemed like she was the only one who wasn't petrified. She ran through the fireplace room and flung open the front door. The cat saw the opening and shot through it. He skidded off the front gallery right into the mouth of Spud's feist Snuffy. Snuffy piled into him and got sent rolling and screeching across the yard.

The tomcat leaped over the yard fence and headed for the woods, with Rock and Drum hard at his heels and baying loud.

Inside the house, Blackie stood wide eyed, wiping his bloody hand across his shirt front. "Why—why the fool thing!" he apologized. "I was just a-pranking. I never—"

His voice trailed off to nothing, leaving his mouth hanging open.

Fiddling Tom's woman stepped to the door and looked into the fireplace room. She uttered a low moan and darted inside. In a little while, she came back with a shard of plaster of Paris in each hand, a look of grief and terror in her soft brown eyes.

"It's broken!" she cried. "Oh, Tom, our 'God Bless Our Happy Home' is broken! Oh, that's a *bad* sign!"

She turned and looked straight at Blackie, with that awful look still in her eyes. "My Tom, he give it to me the day we was married. He told me it was our good-luck piece. And now it's broken!"

Blackie's glance shifted quickly away from Fiddling Tom's woman. It darted down to his bloody hand, fell to the floor, lifted to Dony, then slid on past. He reached for the hole in his pants and started twisting a finger around in it.

"Well, I was just a-pranking," he said guiltily. "Never one time figured that fool tomcat to go crazy!"

Fiddling Tom's woman gave Blackie a blank stare and set the broken plaque gently down on the table. She turned on her heel and walked blindly out of the room. We heard her fall onto the bed in the room where me and Spud had slept and then we heard her deep sobs muffled in the bed quilts.

Fiddling Tom put down his forkful of gobbler breast. He got up and quietly followed his woman into the dark room.

"Now, don't take on so, honey," he said! "Nothing lasts forever!"

Dony looked at Blackie, her face sober. "I think you better go now," she told him.

"But I was just a-pranking," Blackie said. "I never—"

"Go on," Dony said, and the way she said it didn't leave any room for argument.

Blackie looked at me and Spud. He shrugged his shoulders and went into the fireplace room and hunted up his hat and gun. He stopped at the front door and looked back. "Well," he said, "I hate to just eat and run."

Dony said nothing.

Blackie pulled his old hat down low over his eyes and said to me and Spud: "Git the chopping ax and the lantern. I reckon we better go."

The dogs had the wild tomcat treed up a big elm down at the river. We went down there, and Blackie fussed at Rock and Drum till they quit baying and followed us on up the stream.

The moon wasn't up yet and the woods were dark; the only light came from the big pools of water in the river. Blackie walked with his head down, silent, in a deep study.

"The trouble with womenfolks," he grumbled finally, "is how they can git so stewed up and kilt over a little of nothing. That's how come, I reckon, I never takened no stock in 'em. Plague take it, I just aimed to prank a little with that old fool cat!"

I couldn't help feeling bad at what all had happened. I hated to see Fiddling Tom's woman all broken up about losing her "God Bless Our Happy Home." I'd sure planned big on getting to see Mexico Jesus who'd been scalped by a panther. I hadn't got to finish my turkey supper, either, and I was feeling a little empty. Most of all, I hated to leave that black hound-pup of Dony's. I'd never had a dog to take up with me like that before—not a one-man dog.

But I was glad, too; because now, after what all had happened, I didn't much think Blackie would go back to Fiddling Tom's house and maybe take up with Dony again.

10

I WAS dreaming about an army bugle. It kept calling and calling, faint and faraway at first, but clear and sweet. It came nearer and clearer, until the cliff echoes finally caught up the high, clear notes, flinging them back at each other.

Rock growled a low warning. Drum leaped to his feet and gave a short bark. I sat up in bed, wide awake and with every nerve straining to catch the next call of the bugle.

Around me the woods lay quiet in the moonlight, gripped in a hushed waiting. Even the rushing sound of the water tumbling over the river shoal crossing seemed quieter.

The leaves rustled and Blackie spoke in a low voice. "It's a hound-dog," he said, "trailing us up."

I twisted around to find Blackie sitting up in his bed under the wagon, his bushy hair full of shattered leaves.

"Been listening at him for a good long spell now," he said. "He ain't missed a twist or turn we made coming up that river canyon!"

The bugle called again, as high and clear and sweet sounding as it had been in my dreams. It was right at us now, just out yonder the other side of the live-oak grove.

Drum's booming bay lifted. The sound of the bugle faltered and died. Drum, Rock, and Snuffy all charged out through the mass of black shadow that was the grove. They had their hackles up, and were baying loud.

A minute later, their racket changed to whinings and to short barks that was all bluff. They came trotting back through the grove toward us, and behind them, hanging back like a strange dog will, was a half-grown pup, black as the inside of a chimney.

I couldn't believe it at first. I was afraid to. Then Blackie said: "Why, it's that black hound-pup of Dony's!"

Blackie's voice rang shrill with excitement. The pup shied off and circled our camp till he'd located me. Then he ran in, whimpering and whining, and went to licking my face.

I believed it then.

"Now, wouldn't that cock your pistol!" Blackie shouted. "A little old half-growed pup trailing us all the way from Fiddling Tom's. Ten mile if it's a foot, and us a-traveling ever'-which-way, a-mixing up our tracks and follering them hounds of mine all over creation. Why, there's plenty of old trained dogs never could have smelt out that trail. That black pup sure must have a nose on him!"

I couldn't say anything. I was too choked up with all kinds of feelings, shoving and crowding each other inside me. The pup kept licking me in the face and all I could do was hold him in my hands and feel how soft and smooth and warm his hide was and how he was all shaky and shivery with excitement. I was just as shaky and shivery as he was.

"And that trail voice!" Blackie said. "There won't be no varmint in the woods he can't put up!"

Pretty as an army bugle calling, I thought to myself.

Blackie got up and threw a chunk on the live coals of the camp fire. He squatted beside them and started telling me about a man he knew once who'd owned a bugle-voiced hound and another man tried to buy it and couldn't and got mad and tried to shoot the hound for spite and that made the owner mad and he went after the second man with his gun. But I never did learn whether or not he got him, because, for once, I wasn't interested in a hound-dog story. There never could be a told story as good as the one that was happening to me now. A one-man dog had takened up with me. A one-man dog with a voice like an army bugle had singled me out from all the people in the world and trailed me ten miles upriver, just to be with me.

I sat there, not listening to Blackie, and wondered how it was that the pup had picked me. Spud was still asleep, and I was glad. This was a thing too fine to share, right at first. I didn't want to talk about it now. I needed time to get used to it.

I lay back in my quilts and held up the cover for the black pup and he nosed in under and I reached and pulled him down beside me and held him close and warm against my ribs and under my hand I could feel his heart beating strong and steady.

I cried a little then, I was so busting full of happiness; I couldn't hold it. But I kept it quiet so Blackie wouldn't hear, and he was still telling on his story when I went off to sleep.

Something cold and wet and slimy slid across my face and I came up out of a deep sleep, fighting frantically. Beside me, the black pup had already launched an attack with vicious snarls.

My eyes popped open. It was Spud. He was laughing and shouting and trying to yank a yard-long blue cat away from the black pup. The pup had tied onto the tail of the catfish and was shaking it fiercely.

My scare died and I began to feel good at the way the pup had tied into the fish that Spud had dragged across my face. It was the same way Blackie's hounds had pitched in to help him out against Hog Waller.

"He's sure gritty, ain't he?" Spud said. He flopped the catfish over a low limb and tied it up out of the pup's reach. "I never thought no scared-acting pup like that would be gritty."

"He figured that blue cat a danger to Cotton,"

Blackie told Spud. Blackie came from around the wagon, whetting the long blade of his pocket knife on a broken piece of grindstone. "That pup's takened up with Cotton and when a one-man dog takes up with a body, he'll scrap for him to the last drop of blood."

Blackie halted his knife whetting to stare up at the sky, a half-frown creasing his forehead. He turned and glanced quickly behind him, like he'd heard some sound. Then he shrugged and went to where the catfish hung with its gill flaps rising and falling.

He slashed the point of flesh between the gill vents, then pressed the fish's head back till its forked tail drew up in a tight crook and quivered. The bone snapped between Blackie's hands and the blood spurted and ran down the sides of the fish. Blackie dropped the blue cat to let it hang and flop on the string while it died.

Spud said proudly: "Caught him on that bait of jackrabbit liver. Heard my tom turkey bell ringing just at the crack of day, and me'n Blackie went down there and there he was, trying to yank that willer bush up by the roots. Hadn't a-been for that tom turkey bell of mine, he'd a-maybe broke the line before we knowed he was on."

The black pup went over to where the blue cat

dripped blood on the leaves. He sniffed the place and licked at the blood, then came back and sat down beside me.

Blackie kept glancing around nervously. "There's weather a-brewing," he said finally. "Could be we better pull out for home."

Me and Spud both looked at Blackie, too surprised to answer. Blackie glanced at us and then away.

Spud found his voice. "But, Blackie!" he said. "We've got three more days!"

Blackie shook his head. "Look at that sunrise," he said solemnly. "Look at them mare's-tail clouds across the face of the sun, all itchy red in color. 'Red sun in the morning, hunters take warning.' That's a saying my ma had, and Ma knowed a heap about the signs."

I still couldn't say anything. But I knew we couldn't go home. Not yet. Not when I'd just got me a dog to hunt with, like Blackie and Spud. A keen-nosed dog with a voice like an army bugle!

Spud said, "That sunrise don't look no different to me from the others. Just some little old reddish-looking cloud streaks. Ain't no reason to go home just on account of them."

I felt my stomach balling up into a hard knot at the thought of going home—after all Mama'd said about hound-dogs. She'd never let me keep him. I thought: *He isn't really my dog.*

Blackie said: "It ain't just that itchy-looking sunrise. It's an uneasy feeling I got. Like bad trouble's on my trail. Had it all night. It wouldn't let me rest!"

"But we can't go home yet!" My voice came out higher than I'd meant. "We just can't do it!"

Blackie didn't seem to take any notice of what I said. He shook his head again, looking worried. He turned and went to peeling strips of blue hide from the catfish, showing the creamy white flesh underneath. I got up out of bed and set a skillet of hog lard on the fire to heat. Spud sat down and went to skinning on a big possum we'd caught the night before.

We rolled the slabs of catfish in cornmeal and fried them till they were brown and crisp. But seemed like they didn't taste as good as they ought to, not with Blackie so silent and restless, and me and Spud so full of dread about going home.

We finished and Blackie got up and wiped his greasy fingers on his pants legs. He stepped away from camp and stared out down the river canyon, now and then lifting his nose and feeling the air with it like a hound-dog that's winded some varmint a long ways off and can't get it located.

I looked at Spud and he looked at me, both of us

mighty sober. But there wasn't anything to say; all we could do was wait.

Blackie finally reset his hat like he'd made up his mind and came back into camp.

"I don't like it," he said, not looking at us. "It ain't cold enough this morning. We'll go take up them steel traps."

I felt my heart go dead inside me. Spud said, his voice high and shrill as mine had been: "But we don't have to go home on account of a little old spell of weather. Dave Wilson'll take us in if it was to get bad!"

Blackie gave his head a slow shake, then looked off down the river again. "Well, we'll go take up them traps," he said. "Then we'll see!"

We went to gather up the traps and found one missing. We tracked the drag through the tall cedars and over a rocky rise down into a deep canyon. We spent nearly an hour finding where a range hog had finally worked his foot out of the trap and left it wedged between two rocks.

Blackie slung the trap over his shoulder, along with the others. He glanced up at the sky and frowned, shaking his head worriedly.

The sky looked all right to me. There were just a few more mare's-tail streaks than there had been and here and there a buttermilk-looking smear of cloud. But it was a lot warmer, and mighty still, too, so that you could hear things from away off.

Back in the hills to our left an old cow blared and blared again, and down in the river canyon another cow answered her. And a little later we heard a wolf howl lonesome from a ridgetop. Then from somewhere back in a far-off canyon rose the harsh cackle of a laughing owl.

Blackie cocked an ear to each sound and increased his pace till me and Spud were almost in a trot to keep up with him. "Them owls, laughing here in broad daylight," he muttered. "That sure ain't a good sign."

The sound of that laughing owl gave me a creepy feeling, too. It made your hair prickle at the back of your neck. It sounded too much like the laugh of a crazy man. It made me feel little and unimportant out here in these wild hills. I was beginning to feel spooky, myself.

We hurried on down the river and came to the crossing in time to see Dave Wilson out on the gravel bar with a couple of horses. While we crossed on the stepping rocks, Dave hobbled a big ragged, rawboned dun horse and started stripping his saddle off the horse he'd been riding.

Blackie said: "Lordy mercy! Dave's fixing to ride

one of them old fool horses at a time like this!" He
leaped out on the gravel bar and hurried through the
boulders toward Dave and the horses. "Dave!" he
called before he got there. "Don't git on that old
bad horse, Dave. It's a bad time!"

Dave yanked up his saddle cinch and stood away
from the snorty dun. He lifted both eyebrows at
Blackie, like he was fixing to hooraw him.

"It's always a bad time," he said, "when you've got
an old outlaw horse like this dun to ride. But what
makes this time worse'n any other?"

Blackie dumped his shoulderload of steel traps
on the ground and stood bent over, still holding onto
the chains while he looked at Dave.

"It's just—well, plague take it, Dave," Blackie
said defensively, "it's just a feeling I got. I don't like
the signs."

Dave Wilson threw back his head and laughed. His
laugh made me feel easier. But it didn't help the
worried look on Blackie's face.

"Now, Dave, I ain't a jumpy old woman. But I just
got a scary feeling. Something's going to happen;
something bad. We just heered a wolf howl back
yonder on the ridges and one of them old laughing
owls a-jibbering!"

Dave took a squint at the sky. "Sure," he said,

"there's a spell of weather breeding. But that ain't nothing to hinder me from knocking the rough edges off'n this Roman-nosed dun. He'll think the storm's done hit when I climb up in the middle of him!"

He winked at me and Spud like we were in on another joke with him.

That wink and Dave's confident manner melted away the tight feeling I'd had in my stomach since Blackie had first noticed that red sunrise. I grinned and winked back at Dave.

"All right!" Blackie said, daring Dave. "Go on. Git your neck broke. I warned you!"

Dave's grin got bigger. He took a good hold on his hackamore and rocked his saddle to make sure it was all set. The dun snorted.

"Watch him roll the whites of them eyes up," he laughed. "I'll bet that old booger's a-laying for me!"

You could tell Dave wasn't bothered.

He set his hat tight on his head and took the hobbles from the dun's forelegs. He eased a boot into the stirrup, then went up and across, quick as a cat.

"Give us air!" he hollered and slammed his spurs into the dun's shoulders.

The dun bawled and quit the ground like a stump with a stick of dynamite under it. He came down all in a twist and exploded again, then lined out for the

177

river, pitching the hardest and crookedest and fastest I ever saw. And that bellow he had. I never heard a horse bellow like that!

I heard Blackie holler, "Look out!" and then I saw that Dave had lost a stirrup and was down off the dun's ribs. The dun stumbled and piled up with Dave under him, and a terrible fright froze the blood in my veins as the big fighting dun came to his feet again, stomping and kicking, right on top of Dave.

Spud screamed and Blackie said, "Lordy mercy! What'd I tell you!" and ran at the dun, waving his hat. The dun shied off and went into the river, still pitching and bellowing.

Dave lay there among the boulders with his head all bloody and one leg bent away from his body at a horrible angle.

Blackie turned from fighting off the horse and said, "You bad hurt, Dave?" Then he saw Dave's leg and said, "Oh, my goddlemighty damn!" And Dave reached up a hand and wiped some of the blood away from his face and tried to grin at Blackie.

"I guess you was right, Blackie," he said. "I guess it was a bad time." Then he fell back on the rock in a dead faint.

11

I LIT out for town on Dave Wilson's spare horse, riding desperately. I knew you had to ride desperately when you went for a doctor because that's the way the Glenn boys always rode when old lady Glenn took a turn for the worse. Many a time in the dead of night the wild hammering of their horses' hoofs had woke me up and I'd sat up in bed and been thrilled at the sound of how desperately they rode past our house in a race against death. I'd always hoped that sometime I'd get a chance to make a wild and desperate ride for the doctor.

I rode bareback because there hadn't been time to chase down the dun outlaw horse and get the saddle off him, even if any of us could have. We'd been in too big a hurry harnessing my mare to the rig so Blackie and Spud could haul Dave to the house. But I guessed maybe it would look even more desperate if I came tearing into town riding bareback. That way, folks would know how big a rush I was in to get the doctor.

The black hound-pup loped along behind me. He traveled to one side so he could dodge the dust and gravel the horse kicked up. I'd tried to run him back, afraid he couldn't stand such a long and fast run; but he followed me anyhow.

The sun was warm on my back. The pound of the horse's hoofs was a rolling thunder in my ears. Near at hand the brush and trees slid past in a blur, but further out the hills seemed to ride with me.

I rode so desperately that the horse gave out and I had to slow him to a jostling trot that seemed to last for hours. It was the middle of the afternoon, time I reached the edge of town and whipped up for the last mad dash through the streets.

Yard dogs ran out to bark at us and chase along behind and people heard the commotion and stopped whatever they were doing and turned to watch us gallop past. You could tell by the look of growing interest in their faces that they knew my ride was mighty urgent.

I passed where Nita Stringer's folks lived and Nita saw me and came running out of the yard, her eyes wide as saucers. She was hollering: "What is it, Cotton? What's happened?" But I didn't slow up or try to holler back at her. I just kept riding with a grim look on my face. Nita just as well learn now as later that there's some things more important in life than always being able to read and spell all the words in every schoolbook lesson.

At the drugstore, I piled off my horse while he was still sliding to a halt, aiming to hit the ground running, like I'd seen cowhands do. But I'd ridden too long and too fast, or something. My knees felt like rubber; they wouldn't hold me. I came up off my all-fours real quick, though, before anybody much had time to notice, and went running up the outside staircase that led to old Doc Cole's office above the drugstore.

I hammered on the office door and nobody answered, so I hammered again.

"Come in or get out!" old Doc Cole bawled at me.

"But for crying out loud, quit trying to knock the door down."

I opened the door and went in. Doc Cole sat in front of a looking glass, with the slack of his left cheek caught up in his hand and pulled all out of shape. His head was twisted to one side, and he was trying to see which tooth he was grabbing at with a pair of crooked-nosed pincers.

Doc was a big tall, rawboned kind of a man with craggy eyebrows and gray hair and a fierce look in his gray eyes. His eyes were streaming tears now, but he could still glare at me.

"All right, boy!" he barked. "Whatta you want?"

"It's Dave Wilson, Doc," I said. "He's in a bad fix. He let a bad horse get down on him."

"Dave Wilson!" he shouted. "Why, he lives eight or ten miles out of town. I can't go away off down there. I've got a toothache built to fit a horse! And I can't see to pull the confounded thing!"

"But you got to go, Doc!" I said. "Dave's leg's broke. He's in a bad fix!"

"Damnation!" Doc exploded. He slammed his tooth-pulling pincers down on his desk top and got to his feet. "Anybody and everybody else can afford to get hurt or sick; all they've got to do is call the doctor. But who's the doctor to call when he gets sick? Nobody! Hell's fire, they say, what's a doctor doing letting himself get sick, anyway? Doesn't he know his business any better than that!"

The way he went on, shouting and glaring at me that way, had me backing toward the door.

He stopped talking to suck at his sore tooth with a loud smacking sound. "Run down to the wagon yard and tell Rod Jacobs to get my buggy mare hooked up," he said. "We'll have to hurry or that boy's leg will be swelled up like a pregnant woman. Get a move on now, boy!"

I ran down the staircase. A bunch of men were gathered around the horse I'd ridden. They shot curious glances at me and then back at the horse. Tony Goodman, a Devil's River Ranch hand, cut loose with a short laugh. "Damn kid sure must of been bathing his rump," he said.

I looked at the horse, and felt a sudden guilt. He stood spraddle-legged, with his head down, his chest heaving and his flanks quivering. Little rivers of sweat ran down the insides of his legs.

Dave Barker shook his head and turned from the crowd. "Just like a kid," he said. "Run a good horse to death!"

"I was riding for the doctor!" I flared up resentfully. "A bad horse broke Dave Wilson's leg and I had to ride fast for the doctor."

That hushed them up. I reached for the bridle reins and led the horse toward Rod Jacob's wagon yard, the black pup following. But the feeling of shame and guilt stayed with me. Most anybody might have ruined a good horse, riding in for a doctor like that. But I hadn't even thought about it. I'd just been showing off. I didn't feel real proud of myself now.

Rod Jacobs helped my feelings some. He took the horse from me and said: "Now, don't you weary yourself about it, Cotton. You done the best you knowed how. You ride back in the buggy with the Doc. I'll take care of this horse and send him back to Dave Wilson later on."

"Howdy, boy!" a man shouted. I looked up and saw Papa come hurrying through the wagon-yard entrance. "Heard you'd rode in for the doctor. How bad's Dave hurt?" His black eyes were alive with concern.

I was sure glad to see Papa. I didn't know I'd missed him so much till now. I told him about Dave and he shook his head and looked grave. "That's bad, it sure is. I hate to hear that about Dave."

"Is Mama in town?" I asked.

"No, she's getting the sausages ready for smoking," Papa said. "I come to town for seasoning."

I was surprised at how disappointed I was. I sure would like to have seen Mama right then.

The pup reached up to lick my hand and Papa's eyes widened. "Whose hound-pup's that?" he wanted to know.

"He's mine," I said, before I thought. "I mean— he's mine if you and Mama let me keep him." Then I had to tell him the pup really wasn't mine *yet*; Dony hadn't given him to me, but she would. I knew because she'd said she'd be glad to give him to anybody he'd have anything to do with—and he'd takened up with me.

My words got all mixed up the way they came out, and I don't guess I made it very plain. But it didn't seem like Papa was paying much mind anyhow; all his attention was on the pup.

"The spittin' image of my old Nigger dog!" he said in a hushed voice. "I never seen the beat of it!"

"Can I keep him, Papa! Can I keep him if Dony'll give him to me?" It popped out before I remembered how Papa hated to be begged.

But Papa still wasn't hearing me. He was fingering one horn of his mustache and staring at the pup with a recollecting look in his eyes.

185

"That old Nigger dog!" he was saying. "Best dog there ever was. Best friend a kid ever had." Papa wasn't talking to me. I knew that by the sound of his voice and the look in his eyes. He wasn't talking to anybody, unless it was the boy he'd been twenty years ago.

Doc Cole, wearing his black hat and his long black coat, rounded the corner of Stillman's grocery store, taking fast, wide-apart steps. He packed a medicine case in one hand and a quart bottle of whisky in the other. He was hollering at Rod Jacobs, wanting to know if his mare and buggy were ready.

I wished he hadn't come so quick. I wished I had more time to make Papa see I had to have the dog.

"I got to keep him, Papa!" I said frantically. "He's a one-man dog. He won't stay with nobody else. He won't be no good without me! That's what Blackie and Dony and Fiddling Tom all say!"

Papa's mind came back from wherever it'd been and the look in his eyes changed. "You know how your mama feels about dogs," he said.

Rod Jacobs had the mare and buggy out now and Doc Cole was climbing in and shouting: "Git in this buggy, boy, if you're riding with me."

I turned, blinded with tears, to lift the black pup into the back of the buggy. It wasn't any use. Papa didn't understand. Or if he did, he knew he couldn't make Mama see it.

Then I felt Papa's hard hands under my armpits and the surprising strength of him as he gave me a boost up into the buggy beside old Doc Cole.

"Now, you take care of yourself, boy," he said, and added gently: "And take care of that Nigger pup!"

Doc Cole slapped the mare on the back with a rein and we left the staring crowd that had gathered at the wagon yard. We went spinning out of town at a mile-eating trot.

Doc Cole said: "Boy, did you ever have a rotten tooth?"

I shoved the dog worries out of my mind and looked at him. Tears were streaming out of his eyes again, but I couldn't tell if the tooth was making them or the whisky he'd been drinking ever since we'd left town. I'd tasted some whisky once and I knew how hot it was.

"Yes sir," I told him. "It was a baby tooth Mama said I rotted eating candy. But it never hurt much and I wouldn't let her pull it."

"Wouldn't let her pull it?" Doc said. "How'n the hell did you get it out?"

"I never got it out," I said. "I et it."

"Ate it!" Doc Cole snorted and turned a surprised look on me.

"Yes sir," I said. "I was eating a big bait of Mama's canned peaches and felt something scratch my throat on the way down and thought it was a scrap of peach seed hull. But when I stuck my tongue up to see if my tooth was still sore, there wasn't anything there but a big gap; so I knowed I'd et it!"

Doc Cole threw back his head, and his bawling laugh rang out above the fast clip-clop of the buggy mare's hoofs on the hardpan. He laughed too long, seemed to me, just to be laughing about my swallowing a loose tooth. I guessed the whisky was making Doc a little drunk.

He hushed and took another drink, then sat there chuckling. Suddenly, he grunted, clutched his jaw, and swore.

"Why don't you pull it?" I said. "I'd a-let Mama pull mine if it'd been hurting like that."

Doc grunted. "You're overlooking a mighty important fact in this case," he said soberly. "I haven't got a Mama any more. Been dead these forty years. And, old fool that I am, I'm just now beginning to appreciate her." He turned his head and stared off into the brush and timber sliding past us. Finally, he said fiercely: "Why can't a boy appreciate his mother while he's still got her! Why in the hell does he have to wait till she's dead and gone?"

He turned on me, glaring. "Can you tell me that?" he shouted. "Can you tell me why a boy's always got to be so busy chasing rainbow ideas and damn-fool ambitions that he never gets around to loving his mother till it's too late?"

"No sir," I said quickly.

I wished he wouldn't shout at me like that. It scared me. It made me feel bad about Mama, too, and I thought maybe I didn't get around to loving Mama like I ought to.

But then, Mama wouldn't let me have a dog. She couldn't expect me to love her like I would if she'd let me have a dog . . .

My thoughts switched to Doc Cole's aching tooth again. "Look," I said. "One time when Spud had a loose tooth, he tied a string on it and tied the string to a door and then shut his eyes till I'd slammed the door shut! The tooth came right out and Spud said it didn't hurt but just a little."

"Fine!" Doc Cole said with heavy sarcasm. "Now, you just show me the door with a string on it out here in these woods."

I reached into my pocket and pulled out a long

fishing cord wrapped around a cork float. "I got the string," I said.

Doc Cole gave me and the string an impatient look and tilted his bottle toward the setting sun.

"And I got an idea," I said suddenly. "We could use a buggy wheel!"

"Hup! What's that?" Doc lowered his bottle and stared at me.

"We could tie the string to the buggy wheel," I said. "I bet that'd pull it out."

Doc Cole hauled back on the reins. "Who-aa!" he called to the mare, bringing her to a full stop. "An inspiration, boy," he shouted, his big gray eyes shining with sudden interest. "A God-given inspiration. Hand me that fishing string!"

I gave him the string, a little reluctant now. Maybe my idea wouldn't work. Maybe Doc was too drunk to know what he was doing and would hurt himself bad. But I didn't know how to stop him. Doc wasn't the kind of a man a kid could argue with.

He tied a loop in the string. He pulled a slip noose through the loop and fastened it around a jaw tooth, wincing and swearing as he drew it up tight. Then he had me get out and measure off the right distance and tie the other end of the string around the front wheel of the buggy.

"Now, get back in here and take these lines," he ordered. "Get yourself that buggy whip and when I holler ready, you rap that mare a good one. My old teeth are the long-rooted kind that'll need a hell of a yank to loosen."

I got back into the buggy and caught up the reins. I reached and got the buggy whip, half anxious to see if my idea would work, and half scared it wouldn't.

Doc Cole took a drink and braced himself in the buggy seat. He leaned his head back till the fishing line was tight.

"All right, boy," he said. "Cut her a good one!"

I cut her a good one. The startled mare lunged ahead, breaking wind with a loud report.

Doc yelled. His head jerked forward against his stiffened neck, then whipped back. I saw the tooth go whizzing past my face to strike the mare on the rump. Then Doc's big hands clutched the reins over mine and he was hauling the runaway mare down, shouting "Who'aa! Who-aa, now, Nancy girl."

He held the mare down and talked her into a trot and finally brought her to a halt. He spat a mouthful of blood over the wheel and climbed out of the buggy. The tooth was still tied to the string; it lay beside the wheel, all messed up with trash and road dirt.

Doc bent and picked it up. He loosened the string and wiped the tooth clean against his shirt front. He held it up for me to see.

"Clean!" he said. "Clean as a whistle!" He was as wide eyed about that tooth as I would have been if I'd found a ten-dollar gold piece somewhere.

He reeled a little and caught at the buggy wheel for support. "Boy," he said, staring hard at me, "you're a genius. A confounded, double-damned genius! By glory, I've put in a lifetime of study and practice and never in the history of dentistry and medical science did I hear of so simple and successful an operation. Here, let me shake your hand!"

He pocketed his tooth with one hand and with the other reached and crushed my fingers. Then he spat out another mouthful of blood, picked up his bottle, and turned it up. The raw liquor gurgled down his throat like branch water rattling over rocks.

"Nancy!" he shouted, when he'd climbed into the buggy again. "Get up, Nancy. All we got to do now is set a broken leg!" And he started shouting a song about Molly had a wooden leg, so did Sal!

192

12

WE CROSSED the river under an overcast sky. The air was still warm—too warm for wintertime. Almost warm enough for summer. Dark was coming on and around us the hills were fading in the gray light. We drove up the narrow canyon road, where the owls in the dark tops of the live oaks looked down on us, jeering and cackling till it made me jumpy. We pulled up in front of the old gray stone house and found that word of Dave Wilson's accident had already been spread.

Three wagons and two buggies stood in the open spaces in front of the yard. The harness was laid back on the wheels of the vehicles and the work animals were tied up and eating out of the beds. Three saddled horses stood hitched to the yard fence posts.

It was too warm for a fire, but there was one built up out in the yard. I guessed the men had just built it for something to gather around and spit into. The men all wore grave looks on their faces and talked in low-pitched voices, like you do where there's bad sickness in the house. They had out their whittling knives to keep their hands busy while they talked. Some shaved on soft cedar sticks; others casually stabbed their knife blades into the soft yard dirt.

Doc Cole said, "Whoa," and the men all rose to their feet. Ples Newton came out to say howdy and to unhook and feed Doc's mare. The rest of the men stood in their tracks and looked respectful.

Doc climbed down out of the buggy, taking his bottle with him. The bottle was half empty now, but Doc could still walk. "Bring in my pill bag, Cotton," he told me and started toward the house.

I picked up his pill bag and followed, wondering

how news like this made the rounds so fast. Ples
Newton there, he lived fifteen miles upriver. None of
the Wilsons could have had time to get him word.
Yet here he was. And Sol Fikes and his brother Terminus—they were from the Salt Branch country,
twenty miles to the south. Somebody else was coming
up the canyon road right now; I could hear the lum-
bering rattle of the wagon and the harsh, ugly
laughter of the disturbed owls. How could they have
learned so fast about Dave's getting his leg broken?

I guessed a body got hurt or took to his sickbed,
and his neighbors learned it by instinct and came to
set up.

I followed close on Doc Cole's heels, self-conscious
under the steady stares of the men, but proud to be
in on such big doings. Spud came around the corner
of the house and stood and looked at me like he
would a stranger. I looked back at him the same way.
It seemed queer that a thing like this could make
people as close together as me and Spud feel like
strangers, but it did.

Doc's step was heavy on the front gallery, and at
the sound of it there was a sudden hush to the con-
fused murmur of woman talk on the inside. Everybody stopped talking except Aunt Cindy Ferguson.
Aunt Cindy was deaf as a rotten stump, so she always

talked at the top of her voice so she could hear what she was saying.

"You take the time," she was saying, "when the dogs let that bad bar' hog git to my man over on Dead Man's Holler and cut him up so bad. Why, he crawled better'n a mile on his all-fours, spouting a stream of blood ever' step of the way!"

Grandpa Wilson pulled open the door just as Doc was reaching for the latch and that threw Doc off balance. He came close to falling through on his face.

"Come in, Doc," Grandpa said. "I got Dave likkered up good so he can stand a leg-setting."

Grandma Wilson's quarreling voice came from inside the room. "A fine way to send your boy to his Maker, his breath foul with likker."

That scared me. I knew Dave had to be suffering something awful, but I wouldn't have thought he was ready to die yet.

We went inside. All the neighbor womenfolks had gathered there, watching Dave suffer. They were telling tales about other people getting thrown from bad horses and dying from mad-dog bites and poisoned snakes and the like.

Dave lay on a steel-frame cot, wallowing and groaning on his bed quilts. His woman Rachael sat in a chair beside him; she was trying to hold him still and keep his swelling leg laid out straight. She glanced up as we came in and the look she gave Doc Cole made a lump rise up in my throat.

I guess Doc had seen lots of looks like that; it didn't seem to bother him. He came around and laid a hand on Dave's leg and went to joshing him.

"Hello, Dave," he said, "can't you ride the bad ones any more?"

Dave rolled over onto his back and looked up at Doc, his face gray and sick looking in the yellow lamplight. "Ride him, hell!" he stormed out suddenly. "How you gonna ride one upside down?"

Doc laughed and behind us Grandma Wilson called out sharply: "Watch your cussing, Dave. The Lord's a-listening at ye!"

She turned and looked sorrowfully around the room. "It do look like," she said, "that a body on their deathbed could keep from cussing."

Grandpa Wilson grabbed up a chair and hammered it against the floor. "Woman!" he shouted. "Will you bridle that jaw! A man don't die of a broke leg. It's the confounded whining and nagging of womenfolks that kills him off. Now, you let the boy cuss if he wants to. The way he's hurting, he's got a right to cuss!"

He stood and glared at Grandma till she hunched

197

her fat shoulders and drew her head down between them like a terrapin pulling back inside its shell.

"It's a good clean break," Doc said after a minute. "Dave's lucky there."

Dave said thickly, apologizing: "I'd a-rode him, Doc, hadn't a-been for that godawful bellering he let out. Scared me loose from the saddle, that bellering did."

"Fetch me three-four stout men in here, Cotton," Doc said, setting down his whisky bottle and reaching for his pill bag.

I turned to go outside, and Dave said again, "Just that godawful bellering. That's what shook me loose!"

It gave me the creeps to hear Dave talking half out of his head like that. Him lying there dog drunk and with a broken leg. But I guessed when a body had a broken leg, he needed whisky or something to kill the hurt.

The Dooleys from down on Squaw Creek were getting out of their wagon as I stepped off the front gallery—old Grizzly Dooley, his woman Sissy, and his three grown girls, Dolly, Jewel, and Mamie. I'd heard about the Dooley girls; Mama'd said they were all too good looking—that they were bound to go to the bad.

Grizzly reached back under his spring seat and lifted out three brown jugs stoppered with corncobs. "I brung along a little of my own making," he said, "just in case Dave's folks run short. Ain't no medicine as healing, I always claim, as good home-made whisky."

He looked at each man in the yard separately, daring any of them to dispute his words. Nobody did.

I told the men that Doc Cole wanted four of the stoutest on the inside, and Grizzly came in the yard and set his jugs down, away from the heat of the fire, and went on in the house, trailed by his womenfolks. Sol and Terminus Fikes followed them. The rest of the men hesitated, shooting nervous glances at each other.

Blackie looked at Grizzly's jugs a minute, his face flushed like maybe he'd been sampling some of the painkiller Grandpa had been feeding Dave. "Well," he said, "I brung Dave in without a drink. I reckon that with a couple of bracers, I can shorely handle him again."

He went over and took a long drink out of a jug, wiped his mouth with his jumper sleeve, and said: "You lead the way, Cotton."

The womenfolks stared round eyed and fearful while Doc showed the men how to get hold of Dave.

He put one at each of Dave's arms and two on his good leg and told them: "Now, hold him steady till I can slip the edges of the bone back in place."

Dave lay with his eyes shut and his mouth open till they got their handholds on him, then he roused up.

"I tell you," he said wildly, "it was just that godawful bellering. That's what throwed me."

Doc said, "All right, now, hold what you got!"

Rachael's face turned white. She got up and hurried off into the kitchen.

Doc Cole lifted Dave's leg and gave it a sudden hard, twisting pull. That brought Dave up out of his drunken stupor, fighting and roaring like a bull. With a heaving twist of his body, he slung Terminus Fikes clear across the cot above him.

Terminus' heels went high and caught Sol under the chin, knocking him loose from his hold on Dave's other arm. The brothers piled up out in the middle of the floor.

Doc let go of the broken leg and bawled out angrily: "Dammit, if four of you can't keep him from knocking out the last of my old rotten teeth, then call in some more."

Dave fell back, groaning, and the Fikes boys got to their feet, looking wide eyed and sort of sheepish.

Ples Newton came in with one of the Scully twins and took hold of Dave and just then the oldest Dooley girl, Jewel, screamed, "Don't do it again! I just couldn't stand it!" And then she fell across Grandma Wilson's lap in a faint.

Grandma screamed, "Oh, my Lord, she's fainted! What'll I do?" And Doc Cole said, "Hell's fire, leave her lay. Maybe she'll keep her mouth shut for a minute now." Then he turned to the men and said, "Now, I want him held down this time!"

Doc had been pretty drunk when we came in, but you could look at his face and tell that he was cold sober now.

The men gripped Dave's arms and legs again and one sat on his chest. The sweat popped out on their faces and you could see the fright in their eyes when Dave roused up and went to fighting again.

But they were too many for him this time. Dave couldn't get loose. His face turned purple with the hurt and the strain. He lay there and fought and cussed Doc Cole.

"Pull!" he roared at Doc. "Goddammit, pull it off! Had my old six-shooter here, I'd plant a ball square between your eyes!"

Doc Cole didn't pay him any mind. He gave the

broken leg another yank. There was a muffled grating sound of bone rubbing bone and Doc grunted.

Dave cried out hoarsely, then slumped, all the strength draining out of him, leaving him limp in the gripping hands. The whites of his eyes rolled up.

Grandma Wilson leaped up out of her chair. "Lord, ye've taken him!" she shrieked. "Oh, Lord have mercy upon the sinful soul of my poor grand-baby. Oh, Lord, don't blame him for coming to you with a skinful of foul drinking whisky. It was his blaspheemus grandpa what poured it down him. That's the one you want to punish!"

I heard gasps and groans behind me and I thought: *He's dead!* Then Doc shouted at the top of his voice: "Fontel! Come shut up these fool women before I faint, too!" And here came Grandpa Wilson, rushing out of the kitchen where he'd been with Rachael, his black eyes blazing. "Dry up!" he shouted, louder even than Doc. "Confound it, dry up that racket till Doc can get done with the job!"

The hollering and moaning chopped off like you'd cut it with a knife. All but Aunt Cindy's mournful voice.

"I helped to lay 'em out," she was saying. "As purty a pair of corpses as you ever laid eyes on. Oh, it was a heartbreaking sight if I ever seen one! Her, done in her coffin and not a day over sixteen. And clutching to her bosom that little bundle of shame!"

Doc Cole dragged up a chair so he could sit in comfort while he went to binding the splints on Dave's leg. I knew for sure then that Dave hadn't died, that he'd only fainted, so I quit the room on the run. I pushed through the knot of popeyed men jamming the doorway and just barely made it to the edge of the gallery in time. I was sure sick.

The men who'd helped to hold down Dave came out. They went and stood around the fire, nervous and jumpy, glad to be done with a mean job they'd hated to tackle in the first place.

Grizzly Dooley picked up a jug and started passing it around. Each man took a long pull before passing it on. The jug kept making the rounds till when Grandpa Wilson called from the front door.

"Dave's come out of it and resting easy," he said. "Y'all can wash up for supper."

It took four shifts at the table to feed us all, because more and more folks kept coming in. There wasn't anything much but scraps by the time me and Spud got a place. I could tell that Spud left the table hungry, but after the sick spell I'd had, all I could do was just sort of pick at my grub, so it didn't much matter to me.

Out the back door, I came on Grandpa Wilson getting after Rachael for not cooking up more. Rachael's voice was tight when she answered. She claimed she'd cooked up everything in the house except that new barrel of flour that had to do the winter and she didn't know what on earth she'd feed the folks for breakfast. You could tell by the sound of her voice that she was too heartsick and worn out to care.

Grandpa loved her up then and told her not to worry, that he'd round up some of the menfolks to butcher a shoat before daylight. But that only made Rachael feel worse.

"...attening shoats, Pa Wilson!" she cried ". They're for my baby money. You can't butcher my fattening shoats!"

"Well, now, honey," Grandpa said uneasily, "in a case like this, I dunno. Was it daylight, I could maybe go knock over a buck deer or a turkey gobbler. But we're string-halted. We got to have meat before daylight."

But Rachael wouldn't have it. "You can't do it, Pa!" she told him desperately. "You can't butcher my fattening shoats. Like it is, I don't know how we're going to pay Doc Cole for this trip; but I'm not going to have him owning my baby when it comes. Not my baby!"

She wheeled suddenly and disappeared into the dark behind the house.

Grandpa Wilson stood for awhile with his head bent, running his fingers through his thin white hair. Then he headed for the yard fire where the men were squatting around and tapping Grizzly Dooley's jugs again. Grandpa picked up a jug and took a long pull, stopped to get his breath, then took another. He passed it on to the next man and squatted down in the circle of men, where he'd be in line when the jug came back around.

Another wagon reached up outside the yard and t   "Not out. There in the dark, y   out. "who it was. But when they c   the yard where the fire lit up their faces, I saw it was Fiddling Tom and his womenfolks and a dark, squat man with skin like dried leather. The man's eyes were soft and dark and had an odd slant to them.

Sight of Dony made me remember the black pup. I'd thought I'd never forget him, even for a minute, but during that leg-setting, I sure had. I looked around real quick. He was right behind me, ready to come up and lick my hand and let me pat his back the minute he saw I was looking for him.

Then I recollected he'd belonged to Mexico Jesus and I knew right off the dark man with Fiddling Tom had to be Mexico Jesus, the man the panther had scalped!

Dony and Fiddling Tom's woman went straight toward the house. Fiddling Tom and Mexico Jesus came up to stand by the fire. Everybody got up and shook hands with Fiddling Tom, but just howdied Mexico Jesus and let it go at that, him being a Mexican.

Seemed to me I'd rather shake hands with a panther-scalped Mexican than with any white man I knew. But that wasn't the way things went. I eased around the crowd and got close to Mexico Jesus, hoping he'd maybe lift his hat and I'd get to see the scar under his coarse gray hair.

At the door, Dony glanced back over her shoulder at Blackie before she went in, but Blackie didn't take any notice of her. He tilted a jug and passed it to Fiddling Tom.

"You and Mexico Jesus bring your music boxes?" he asked.

Fiddling Tom nodded. "They're in the wagon,"

he said. "I never can tell when I'm liable to run across a tune that needs playing."

He drank and passed the jug to Mexico Jesus. The panther-scalped man held it and looked uncomfortable.

Grandpa Wilson said: "There's a tomater can stuck on the fence post behind you, Mexico."

Mexico Jesus turned and went to pour himself a drink into the tomato can.

Grizzly Dooley said: "Tom, the way you offer to let that greaser drink out of the same jug, you'll have him expecting to eat at your own table, same as a white man!"

Fiddling Tom turned a solemn look on Grizzly. "He's welcome at my table any time," he said. "He can take that git-tar and second a fiddle better'n ary man in the country!"

"That don't make him white," Grizzly insisted.

"A man's a man," Fiddling Tom said emphatically, "irregardless of his skin color. It's what's in his heart that counts. And you can tell what's in Mexico Jesus' heart by his music."

Grizzly Dooley looked baffled. Blackie got up from his squat and turned his back end around to the fire.

"I could stand to hear a good tune knocked off right now," he said.

Terminus Fikes nodded. "It'd go good with this here drinking whisky. Help to take the bad taste of that leg-setting out of a man's mouth."

"Some of us," said Grandpa Wilson, "has got to butcher a shoat!"

"Tonight!" Grizzly Dooley looked surprised.

"It's butcher in the dark," Grandpa said, "or have some lank bellies when this drinking whisky wears off about daylight."

Fiddling Tom looked suddenly worried and a little nervous. He glanced at Mexico Jesus. Mexico Jesus nodded and showed pearl-white teeth in a shy grin.

"Well," Fiddling Tom said, "I guess me'n Mexico Jesus could finger you boys a little tune to keep you company while you're at it." He said something in Spanish and Mexico Jesus went out to bring in the fiddle and guitar.

Grandpa Wilson told Blackie to get his .22 gun to do the hog killing with and told Spud to get the lantern. "I'll rustle up the butcher knives," he said. "We'll skin him to save heating water for scraping the hair."

I followed Grandpa around to the kitchen door,

hoping maybe there was a scrap of something left to eat—I was getting hungry again now. But when I looked in the door, Dave's woman Rachael had the table clean, so I didn't go in. I just stood at the door.

Rachael watched Grandpa gathering up his butcher knives and putting them in a tin water bucket, and her face got grim.

"Pa Wilson," she said, "what're you fixing to do with them butcher knives?"

Grandpa stepped back from the table, frowning regretfully. "Now, Rachael," he said, "these is our own borrowing neighbors, come to set up with Dave in his trouble. Dave wouldn't want 'em to go hungry!"

Panic leaped into Rachael's eyes. "But, Pa!" she protested, "this is my first-born." I could see the tears fixing to come."

"Rachael!" Grandpa's voice was stern with reproach. His bright eyes snapped.

Rachael stared at him for a long time. The tears came and spilled down her cheeks and she didn't wipe them away. Finally, she nodded, slumped into a chair, and buried her face in her drying rag.

Grandpa Wilson patted her shaking shoulders. "Now, honey," he said softly. "There's times when you're whupped before you're started. You can work and fight and strain, and still you can't win. It's sure hell to take, but you have to take it!"

He stood looking down at her a little bit, then left her there, and we went off to butcher the shoat while Fiddling Tom and Mexico Jesus squatted by the yard fire and filled the warm night with pretty music.

13

THE butchering was done. In the pale yellow light of a smoky lantern, Ples Newton was hanging the fresh meat to the smokehouse rafters.

"Might as well do our lard rendering on that yard fire," Grandpa Wilson said, then cackled. "Closer to the drinking jugs!"

He and Grizzly Dooley each hooked a finger in

the ear of a cast-iron washpot and started around the house.

Grandpa called back over his shoulder to me and Spud: "You young squirrels bring them buckets of hog fat and we'll soon have us some crackling meat."

We picked up the buckets of hog fat and followed the men around the house.

Beside the fire, Fiddling Tom and Mexico Jesus were making faster music now and in the wavering light of the flames, I could see couples dancing on the front gallery.

"Be dog, now, that's an idee!" Grandpa Wilson exclaimed.

He and Grizzly set the pot up beside the hot fire. Grizzly slipped a rock under one leg to balance the pot while Grandpa poured in the first bucket of hog fat. The fat started popping and frying almost at once.

Terminus Fikes came off the gallery, leading one of Grizzly's girls by the hand. "You don't reckon it'll weary Dave none," he asked soberly, "us doing a little rug cutting out here on the gallery?"

"Why, it'll cheer him!" Grandpa declared, tapping his foot to the music. "Nothin' Dave'd like better than to know his friends and neighbors was having theirselves a good time."

Terminus Fikes nodded: "Blackie said you'd figure it that way," he said. "We just wanted to be sure we wasn't wearying him none."

Grandpa stepped away from the fire and lifted a jug. "Keep right at it," he said. "But watch me'n Grizzly here. Was we to take us a notion to grab up a young filly apiece and rattle our old bones some, you young bloods'd see some caper cutting like it was meant to be done!"

He gave Grizzly's girl a knowing wink that had her still laughing after Terminus had led her back on the gallery.

Somebody had brought out a chair for Fiddling Tom. He sat tilted back in it and fiddled with his head thrown back and his eyes shut, lifting one foot all the way off the ground to stomp it at each beat of the music.

Mexico Jesus sat close by on a sawhorse, hunched low over his ringing guitar. His little black eyes darted this way and that, not missing a thing. He caught me watching him and flashed me a quick white-toothed smile that had in it something warm and secret, and I knew if I got a chance to ask him, he'd show me his scar where a panther tore his scalp loose.

The dance tune he and Fiddling Tom played was

a catchy thing that kept tugging at me, rousing up a lot of yearnings for I didn't know what.

Grizzly Dooley said suddenly, past a jug he held slanted toward his mouth: "Dangamighty, Fontel! Who's that she, cheeking up to Blackie Scantling yonder?"

I peered with Grandpa Wilson at the shuffling mass of couples on the darkened gallery.

"Where?" said Grandpa.

"There on the far end of the gallery," Grizzly said. "That'n what looks like she's been melted and poured into that shiny red dress!"

I located Blackie by his curled-up ducktail and stared at the big yellow-haired woman dancing with him.

"Why, that's Hog Waller's woman," Grandpa told Grizzly. "A new un. Third or fourth—I disremember which. There sure ain't nothing wrong with where she bulges and curves, is there?"

"Nor with the way that twisting be-hind fills her dress out," Grizzly declared. "Dangamighty!"

"It's enough to set the dogs to howling," Grandpa agreed. "Now, if I was ten year younger—!"

Blackie swung his partner to the edge of the crowd and the fire blazed up just then, throwing the light on them, and I looked at the woman who made

Grandpa wish he were ten years younger. She was big and tall and yellow haired and had a sleepy look in the big eyes she kept slanting up at Blackie. Her red dress was pretty, but it was sure tight and short and left a lot of white skin bare at the top.

Grizzly Dooley gave a low whistle. "Where'd Hog cabbage onto a high-roller like that?" he wanted to know.

"Santone," Grandpa said. "You know Hog. He goes for them big-town women. They cost him high and they don't last long, but while they're with him, Hog sure beds in high cotton!"

Blackie had on his party clothes now. I didn't know when he'd left the hog killing to change, but there he was, in tan shoes, a candy-striped shirt and a checked suit. He had his black hair all combed and slicked down now, and he'd shaved clean, too. He sure did look fine. You'd never have taken him for a coon hunter with a hole in the knee of his borrowed pants.

But somehow, I didn't like him so well. I'd a whole lot rather seen him in his old clothes and on a coon trail than all diked out and dancing with Hog Waller's woman. That didn't look good to me, after the run-in we'd had with Hog. It made me uneasy.

Grizzly shook his head. "Now, wouldn't that beat

215

you!" he said. "Yonder's Hog off the end of the gallery, telling it sweet to Birdy Johnson. Be dog, if I
had me a high stepper like Hog's got, I sure wouldn't
waste no time trying to toll a widder woman out into
the dark!"

Grandpa laughed. "Well, you know how it is,
Grizzly. Courting your own woman is like stalking
a tame turkey—ain't no sport to it!"

Grizzly hiccuped and nodded gravely. "That's a
fact," he said. "I never had put no thought on it
that way, but it's sure a fact, all right!"

Fiddling Tom and Mexico Jesus wound up a tune
and in the short silence that followed, a wind came
moaning through the canyon oaks. It was a cold wind
and it hit hard, tearing at the fire and making it leap
and roar. It sent swirling ashes and smoke flying into
the crowd, scattering it. The women hollered and
shrieked, like excited women will, and jammed the
front door of the house, all trying to get inside at
once.

"Dangamighty, Fontel!" Grizzly said, looking up
at the tossing live-oak branches overhead. "We got
us a spell of weather on!"

Fiddling Tom and Mexico Jesus got to their feet
and stood with their backs bent to the wind. They
wrapped their coat fronts around their music boxes
for protection.

"Knowed we had us a howler on the way," Grandpa shouted. He ran to the corner of the yard and picked up a piece of tin roofing. "That old snake-bit leg of mine's been telling me about it for a couple of days now!"

The wind caught against the piece of tin, whirled Grandpa around and off balance. He came stumbling toward us, the wind blowing the tin like a boat sail, dragging him straight into the fire. But Grizzly said, "Dangamighty!" and stepped in and caught the tin in time to save Grandpa from getting dragged right through and burned. Together, they managed to turn the tin edgeways to the wind and clamp it down over the washpot.

"Git us a rock, Spud!" Grandpa called excitedly, then shouted at the crowd on the gallery. "You folks git inside the house. It'll be a mite crowded, but there ain't no bluff to this here norther—it'll freeze your ears off smooth with your head before long!"

Spud found a rock just outside the yard and came packing it in, bent and grunting under the load. I ran and got another, so we could hurry and get inside, too. That wind was getting icy; it cut right through your clothes.

Grizzly turned his coat collar up and told Grandpa to go on inside and build up the fire for his company, that he'd tend the lard rendering till it was done. Grandpa tried to argue, but Grizzly wouldn't listen.

"Just leave me one of them jugs handy," Grizzly said. "It ain't going to be but a little bit till I can drag this pot off the fire!"

So we left him there with a jug and packed the rest inside, where the folks were all milling around, still shivering and talking nervously about the spell of weather that had hit.

Grandpa built up a big fire in the fireplace, then pushed into the middle of the room and hollered for attention. "Don't let this spell bother your partying none," he shouted. "We'll move Dave out into the kitchen to make room for the fiddlers and, by gum, we'll throw us a square dance while she blows. Me, I'll do the calling!"

From his cot, Dave shouted right back at Grandpa. "There ain't nobody moving me nowhere, Pa," he hollered. "This here's my party and I don't aim to miss one whoop or holler of it!"

The crowd parted a little, laughing and hollering at Dave, and I caught a glimpse of him propped up on one elbow, holding a bottle of whisky in one hand.

"This broke leg," he shouted, "it can do its hurt-

ing right here where I can see all the fun, same as
out in the kitchen. Put your fiddlers in the corner
where Granny is and git on with your romping and
stomping!"

Dave's face was beaded with sweat that his woman
Rachael kept wiping off with a rag. Dave was still
dog drunk. You could tell that by his heavy breathing and the roguish cut of his eyes. But the way he
kept grinning and talking up the dance, it was plain
he was having himself a good time—in spite of his
broken leg.

"Line 'em up, Pa!" he called. "Wheel 'em and
deal 'em!" And then he fell back with a big hollering
laugh when the men grabbed up Grandma's chair,
with her still in it, and started packing it into the
kitchen.

Grandma sure did fuss and take on about getting
moved out of her corner next to the fireplace. "Put
me down, you fools!" she shrieked. "Have you all
gone and lost what scattering of brains the Lord give
you!"

But the whisky had the men feeling prankish now;
they laughed and hoorawed Grandma. Ples Newton,
who'd come in from the meat hanging said: "Now,
Grandma, dry up that quarreling and step down out
of your chair. Forty year back, there wasn't a woman

on the Llano could shake a foot with your'n, and I'll bet you can still show plenty of 'em new tricks!"

Grandma tucked her chin at that and said: "Now, Ples, you're jist a-baitin' an old woman with one foot in the grave!" But it was plain that Ples had pleasured her by bragging about how she used to could dance. She hushed right up and got pink in the face and made them set her chair close to the door where she could look through and watch the dancing.

Grandpa dragged chairs and a box into Grandma's corner. He seated Fiddling Tom and Mexico Jesus, and while they tuned up their music boxes again he went into the kitchen and brought out a big cup of cornmeal and scattered it on the floor. Then he hollered for everybody to limber up with another drink.

"Have at it!" he shouted, reaching for the jug he'd had me bring in. He took a drink and his eyes snapped fire and his bushy eyebrows bristled. "Drink 'er down! By gum, we're sarving a free snake with ever' finger of this scamper juice!"

That set the men to yelping and the women to laughing louder and Ples hollered at Grandpa to water that stuff of Grizzly's, that it'd draw blood blisters on a rawhide boot, and Grandpa's eyebrows lifted higher than ever and his face beamed as he got back at Ples.

"Now, don't try to get me drinking she-fashion, Ples," he said. "I ain't putting this fire out with no water!"

He hopped up on a box beside Fiddling Tom, flapped his elbows like a rooster and crowed at the top of his voice.

"Law me!" Grandma said, shaking her head. "When that little old man gits likkered up, he's crazier'n a peckerwood eating stick candy. Ain't he wicked!"

Grandma looked about half proud of how wicked Grandpa was.

"Grab yore partners!" Grandpa shouted and yelped with excitement at the stampede that followed. He crowed again and dragged them into line.

Fiddling Tom and Mexico Jesus cut down on "Cotton-eyed Joe," and Grandpa threw back his head and called at the top of his voice:

> *"Come rain or shine, sleet or snow;*
> *Doc and that Dony gal is bound to go!"*

The crowd went wild, yelping and hollering, stomping their feet, following Doc Cole and Dony, the leaders, through the dance sets as Grandpa called them off.

> *"Walk the shuffle and the Chinese cling,*
> *Elbow twist and the double-L swing!"*

It was sure exciting to watch. Spud and me backed off into the corner next to Dave Wilson's cot, getting out from underfoot, and Dave waved his bottle and shouted: "Swing 'em, now! Swing 'em and wring 'em!"

There in the lead, Dony was sure doing some pretty dancing. Her face was flushed and she talked a blue streak to old Doc Cole, but I noticed that every little bit, her eyes hunted the crowd over for Blackie and that Waller woman.

The music was shrill and sweet. The measured stomping of feet against the floor boards was like drum beats in my ears. I wanted the worst in the world to get out there and dance and holler with the rest of them.

> *"Swing yore partners round and round;*
> *Pocket full of rocks to hold me down!*
>
> *Ducks in the river, going to ford;*
> *Coffee in the little rag, sugar in the gourd!"*

"Swing it!" Grandpa yelled, and beside us, Dave started calling out: "Pla-a-a-ay it purty, Papa Tom. Play it purty now!" And his woman Rachael said,

"Hush, Dave! Hush, now, man. You keep on and you'll maybe hurt that leg all over again."

Dave rolled his eyes up at her and his flushed sweaty face broke into a devilish grin. "Lordy mercy, gal! Wasn't for this old broke leg, I'd be down bellering and pawing the dirt!"

"Please now, Dave!" Rachael begged. But Dave was too drunk and too excited to listen. He kept shouting: "Swing it, chickabiddies!"

Up on his box, Grandpa Wilson called:

> *"Swing 'em early, swing 'em late,*
> *Swing 'em around Sol Fikes' gate!"*

They finished "Cotton-eyed Joe" and, almost without missing a beat, swung into "Turkey in the Straw." Then it was "Dinah Had a Wooden Leg."

It went on and on, getting louder and wilder and faster. Couples played out and stopped to catch their breaths and take on a drink and other couples took their places. The ones not dancing lined the walls, clapping their hands in time to the music.

Gradually, the fun of watching played out for me. I was dead tired from my ride into town. I'd lost too much sleep coon hunting of a night, already. I crawled in under Dave's cot and tried to sleep on the thumping, quivering floor.

I dozed a little—I don't know how long—and

then somebody got to dancing too close to the cot and kicked one of my feet I'd left sticking out. It woke me and I crawled out from under the cot and got up to look around.

Spud was gone and I couldn't see him anywhere, at first, then I saw him at the front door, motioning for me to come there, so I worked my way around the edge of the crowd and squeezed through the door.

"What is it!" I said.

Spud's eyes danced with excitement. "Foller me," he whispered.

He led off around the corner of the house, where the cold wind struck us full force, nearly taking my breath. He stopped at the next corner, held me back out of sight while he took a cautious look around it, then darted across the yard at a fast run.

I ran after him and around to the back of a slab-rock hog pen built against the corn crib. I squatted down beside him, out of the howling wind, and said again, "What is it, Spud?"

"Wait, now!" he whispered. "Keep quiet and listen!"

I sat and listened and when I quit breathing so hard from the quick run, I could hear voices coming from down at the spring. I bent over and looked around the corner of the hog pen. The night had got darker with the coming of the blizzard, but through the clouds the full moon still gave a dim light, and out there apiece, under the waving branches of the live oaks, I could see a man and a woman. The man had his arm around the woman, half dragging her along. The woman was giggling and trying to fuss at him at the same time, pulling back a little, but not much.

"I tell you, that Dony saw us," she said. "I know she did. She's had her eye on you all night. You'd think she owned you!"

"She don't own me," the man said. "Don't no woman own Blackie Scantling!"

"But what if she saw us?" the woman said.

"All right, what of it?" Blackie demanded. "She done had her chance!"

The woman giggled at that, but started pulling back again. "But she might tell," she said. "If she tells and Ed hears about it—well, that Ed, he's mean!"

Blackie gave a short laugh. "Let him come fooling around here and I'll set the dogs on him. They done et the fat seat out of his britches once!"

The woman looked up at Blackie and giggled some more.

They came closer, right up to the corncrib door, then the woman hesitated. "We ought to wait," she said, "till we know for sure she didn't see us."

But Blackie wouldn't listen. "Hush, woman," he said. "We didn't come out here in this dark to argue!" And he caught Hog Waller's yellow-haired woman around the waist with both hands and pulled her, giggling and fussing, into the darkness of the corncrib.

Beside me, I heard Spud snicker.

I got to my feet, all torn up inside with a lot of mixed feelings I couldn't name. I started toward the house, hearing and yet not quite hearing in a lull of the wind the loud chanting call of Grandpa Wilson:

> "Chicken in the bread tray, kicking up dough;
> Granny, will your dog bite? No, by Joe!"

I stopped at the kitchen door and stood for a long time, not wanting to go back inside the house where all the hollering and dancing was. I stood in the cold darkness, listening to the wild singing of the fiddle and the measured stomping of the dancers' feet on the shaking floor boards. Hard stinging pellets of sleet started hissing down through the tree tops and rattling on the roof and biting at my hot face. I wished I knew some place else to go. I felt lost and miserable.

I wanted to see Mama. I wanted to see Papa. I wanted to eat Mama's good cooking and have her tuck me into bed again, even before I was ready. I wanted to hear Papa read the paper out loud to Mama and cuss the Republicans for bringing ruination down on the country. I was tired of strange people and the strange, confusing things they did.

And then from inside the kitchen came a voice so familiar it was like finding an old toy.

"We came just as quick as we could get off. I told Aaron you folks would be needing help at a time like this!"

It was like a Bible-book miracle!

I flung open the door. "Mama!" I cried.

14

MAMA turned from warming her hands over the kitchen stove. "Well, Cotton Kinney!" she said. "What're you doing out of bed this time of night!" Then she gasped and looked quickly at Rachael and her face turned a guilty red.

Rachael said: "There just wasn't any place left in the house for the little fellers to bed down in, Miz

Kinney. I'm ashamed about it, but when men get to whisky drinking, the feelings of their womenfolks don't seem to count!"

Mama pulled off her bonnet and stood looking uncomfortable, trying to smile at me at the same time.

I was so glad to see her I could just barely keep from hugging her neck and telling her. But I didn't want to do that in front of other people, so I just stood and looked through the open door at whirling dancers in the other room.

Papa shoved through the door behind me, grunting under the weight of a tin tub covered over with a white tablecloth. Dony came in right behind him.

"Set it here on the table, Aaron," Mama said, and when he'd done it, she reached and pulled off the tablecloth and began lifting out bowls of baked sweet potatoes, butter, bread, rings of sausage, jars of jelly, and half a big apple pie.

"Just nick nacks," Mama apologized. "Odds and ends that I could scrape together before we got off. Didn't have time to fix anything fittin'."

Just listening to the way Mama always ran down her own cooking made my mouth start watering, almost as much as the sight of the food. I reached for the piece of apple pie.

"Now, son," Mama fussed, "don't eat it all up before anybody else gets a bite!"

"Let him eat, Miz Kinney," Rachael said. "Him and Spud, they didn't hardly get nothing at the supper table. The rest et it up ahead of 'em."

Rachael stopped and bit her underlip to keep it from quivering. She looked worried, like things had got so out of hand she didn't know which way to turn. I guessed it was bad, all right, having to feed your baby-money shoats to this bunch who'd come to set up.

Papa grinned down at me. He reached and caught one of my ears and gave it a twist. "You got around to telling Mama about your Nigger dog yet?"

I looked at Dony, where she sat on the woodbox beside the kitchen stove, being mighty still and quiet for Dony. Her eyes were too big and hollow looking. They stared at us, her eyes did, but it didn't look like they were seeing anybody.

"I guess he isn't my dog," I told Papa. "I guess he belongs to Dony. He just followed me off!"

Dony quit staring at nothing. She took a deep breath, looked at me, and her eyes softened. "He's your dog, Cotton," she said gravely. "He wouldn't take up with Mexico Jesus and he wouldn't take up with me. If he's followed you off, he's bound to be yours."

I felt a sudden wild hope. I had me a dog, a one-man dog with a voice like an army bugle!

Then I looked at Mama and remembered and felt the start of tears stinging my eyes.

"Mama won't let me have him," I said.

Dony looked at Mama in surprise. "Of course she'll let you have him!" she said. "A boy and a dog go together. Like pepper and salt. Like—like husband and wife. If I ever have me some fine boys, they're all going to have dogs!"

There was something heartbreaking about the way Dony said that last. I couldn't help noticing it.

Mama noticed it, too. She started and looked at Dony, then began twisting her bonnet strings around her red hands. "Well," she said, "I just never did hold with a boy's running wild in the woods with a passel of old hound-dogs!" She puckered her lips and stared down at the bonnet strings she twisted.

Papa started to put in, but just then a woman screamed in the next room.

She screamed again and a man's voice lifted harsh and loud. The music trailed off and I heard a man cussing in hoarse anger and a lot of other voices rising, sharp with excitement.

"A fight!" somebody shouted, and Rachael gasped. "I knew it was coming," she said in a scared voice.

"With all that whisky drinking, it was bound to come!"

She started for the door, with Mama and Dony following.

"Lord have mercy!" Grandma Wilson prayed, coming awake. "Lord, don't let them murder a pore old defenseless woman right here in her chair. Don't you do it, now, Lord!"

Papa shoved ahead of the women, telling them to wait a minute. He stepped through the door. I followed close behind Papa, eager to see.

Papa kept shoving through the crowd till it was too tight packed to open. But now I could stand on tiptoe and see what the trouble was.

Hog Waller had his woman and Blackie hemmed up in the far corner of the room and was trying to hit Blackie on the head with a big six-shooter. Blackie had his arms held out in front of his face, dodging the gun.

"Now, don't hit me with that old gun, Hog!" he quarreled. "Look out, now, dang it! You got no call to hit me with that old gun!"

Waller hit Blackie with the gun and knocked him to the floor. A lot of women screamed and Hog's woman cried out: "You've kilt him, Ed! You've kilt him!" Her blue eyes weren't sleepy now.

"Not yet, I ain't," Hog Waller said. "He'll git up if he's got the guts to! But this time he won't have a pack of old dogs to do his fighting."

Papa said: "Let me through here! Let me through!" But nobody moved.

Ples Newton said, "Why can't you fellers take it outside. This ain't no place to settle a difference!"

Hog Waller whirled on him. "Outside, hell!" he bawled. "That's where they started it. I'll wind it up in here!"

Hog was reeling drunk. His red face was beaded with sweat and looked swollen. His thick lips were peeled back in an ugly half-grin. His little eyes were nearly shut but there was a bright hard light in them that made me shiver.

Blackie started getting to his feet. Blood was running down the side of his head. He came up in a half-crouch and tried to duck out of the corner past Hog. But Hog swayed his big body in front of him, swinging up the six-shooter for another lick.

Hog's woman screamed and caught the arm that held the gun. She swung down on it, begging. "Don't hit him no more, Ed!" Her yellow hair was looking mussy.

"Get hold of that gun, somebody!" Papa yelled.

Hog slung his woman loose, slamming her against

the wall. "Shut up!" he shouted. "I'll learn that varmint-chasing tramp to tamper with Ed Waller's woman. I'll learn you to spread your bait around, too!"

Hog's woman stood trapped in the corner with Blackie and there was panic in her eyes. "But it wasn't me!" she cried. "You know me, Ed. You know I wouldn't go for a country rake like this. It's always been big strong men I went for. Like you, Ed!" She slanted her eyes at Hog, but her big red mouth was scared.

Her sweet-talk made Hog hesitate, but he was still suspicious. He stood and stared at his woman.

Papa kept shoving and straining at the jam of people, getting a little closer all the time. I stayed right at his heels.

"You was out," Hog accused his woman. "I missed you. And he was out at the same time!"

"We were both out," the woman admitted. "But we wasn't out together. I just stepped out to get a breath of air. He had him another woman!" She was talking fast.

"All right, who was it?" Hog demanded. "If it wasn't you he had out, who was it?"

"I don't want to tell, Ed," the woman hedged.

"That would ruin some girl's reputation!" She tried to smile at Hog.

"Reputation!" sneered Hog. "Ary woman sorry enough to let that sneaking thing toll her out ain't got no reputation. She ought to be stripped naked and yoked to him and both of 'em drove out of the country with a horse whup!"

"But, Ed!" she said.

"*Who was it!*" Hog's face started getting black. He drew back his big left hand to slap his woman.

"Don't! Don't, Ed!" she screamed. She shrank back against the wall, holding her hands up over her face, and she wasn't pretty any more. "I'll tell!"

"All right, then tell!" Hog said. "I'll learn him to laugh at Ed Waller!" He twisted his head around and his little mean eyes darted over the crowd. His thick lips curled back in a dirty pleased grin.

There was a sudden hush in the close-packed room. The scent of hot, excited bodies got rank and stifling. Everybody stared at Hog Waller's big woman, waiting for her to tell what woman Blackie'd had out.

All the scare seemed to have left her now. She stood up straight and took a deep breath, bulging the front of her red dress. She took her time about searching the room, like maybe she enjoyed keeping everybody waiting as long as she could. Suddenly, she pointed, straight over me and Papa.

"It was her!" she said. "It was Dony Waller he took out to the corncrib!"

That bald-faced lie took my breath. It must have taken the breath of everybody else, too, even if they didn't know it was a lie, because for a second there wasn't a sound in the room except the snapping of the coals in the fireplace.

Then some woman gasped and another one giggled and some man said, "Well, I'll just be damned!" like he thought he'd been cheated out of something.

Every eye was turned on Dony, who stood close behind me, and I turned too, in time to see the surprise whiten her face. I saw the fright that was in her eyes, too, and the slow-coming anger and scorn that took its place as she stared straight back at Hog Waller's woman.

A woman's voice back of Dony said in a half-whisper, "It's what you can expect when you turn a girl loose to run wild."

And then Blackie came up out of his crouch in the corner, looking around wildly, and Hog Waller slammed him across the head with his six-shooter barrel, piling him up on the floor again. Hog roared,

"Lay still, you varmint-chasing son of a bitch. You killed the best sow I've got and laughed about it, but you can't laugh this off. You don't tamper with a Waller girl and live to brag about it!" Then he cocked his six-shooter and backed off, pointing his gun down at Blackie.

It came to me then that he was fixing to kill Blackie and I tried to scream, but nothing came out.

Hog tried to draw a bead on Blackie, but was too drunk to hold it. The gun kept wavering till Papa was in there, clutching Hog's arm, shoving the gun up and away from Blackie. The gun went off with an ear-splitting report. The bullet struck the wall high up in the corner, knocking down a stinging shower of rock chips and plaster as it tore through the ceiling.

Then Papa had the gun and was beating Hog Waller in the face with it, and I knew all at once that my papa was the bravest man on earth. My papa had the nerve to fight a man twice his size. He had the nerve to fight a man nobody else in the room would tackle. He could walk right in and take a man's gun away from him and whip him in the face with it.

I never had felt proud of my papa before, but now I was so proud of him that I thought my aching throat would burst and I went to screaming, "Kill

him, Papa! Kill him!" and started climbing up on
top of people's shoulders, crazy to get in there and
help Papa kill that drunk Hog Waller.

But Papa wasn't trying to kill him. He just beat
him till Hog quit fighting back and fell against the
wall, grunting and groaning like some big bad-hurt
animal, wiping the blood from his face with his big
clawing hands. Then Papa stepped back, holding the
gun in his hand like he didn't quite know what to
do with it. He was breathing hard and his black eyes
were fiery, but when he spoke his voice was quiet
and steady.

"I reckon this can be settled without a killing,"
he said.

Blackie started scrambling up from the floor again.
There was more blood running down the side of his
head now. Blackie had a dazed look in his eyes, like
he wasn't sure what had happened.

Behind me, I heard Fiddling Tom's woman crying. "Tell 'em, honey-baby," she was begging. "Tell
'em it's a lie!"

Dony patted her mama on the shoulder and went
to steady Blackie. She caught him under one arm
and held him, leading him over to Dave's cot, where
she jerked a slip off a pillow and started wiping the
blood from his face. She was a long time in turning

to face the crowd and, when she did, it was with her chin held high and proud and her brown eyes shining.

"I don't know what all this big to-do is about," she said. "What's between me and Blackie is our own business. Blackie's never give me cause to think he won't do right by me!"

Blackie started out of his daze and turned an amazed look on her. Back of me, I heard a bunch of women gasp and one said, "Well, of all the gall!" And then Fiddling Tom's woman flung her apron over her face and stumbled blindly toward the kitchen.

"I knew it," she wailed. "I knew bad trouble was on us when that cat broke my Happy-Home plaque."

Fiddling Tom caught her and loved her up. "Now, wait a minute, honey," he said. "All young things grow up and mate. There ain't nothing been done that a marrying won't fix. You got to recollect, we was a mite eager, too, at the start!"

"But it wasn't Dony!" I said desperately. "I tell you, it wasn't Dony!"

Hog Waller's woman leaped at me like a mad cat. "Shut up, you lying little whelp," she spit out. Her eyes were blazing; she grabbed at my arm.

239

But already Dony had a hand over my mouth and was dragging me toward the front door. "You want to get him killed?" she said in a frantic whisper.

She hurried me on outside and off the gallery. She led me out into the falling sleet, away from the lamplight shining through the windows.

"You mustn't ever tell, Cotton!" she whispered fiercely, holding me tight by both arms and shaking me. "You understand? You mustn't ever let Spud tell. If Hog ever finds out, he'll kill Blackie!"

She stood holding me, breathing hard. Then she said in a soft voice, "He's my man, Cotton. I love him! I don't want him killed."

She hugged me up close, but gentle, patting my shoulder. Her long hair fell across my face, soft and warm and clinging like silk. It had a sharp, clean scent about it, like Mama's hair.

She cupped her hands under my chin and pulled my face up close to hers. "Promise?" she said.

I didn't know what to do. I was all mixed up. Hog Waller's woman had lied. Dony had lied. And if I didn't tell the straight of it, Blackie was trapped. Dony would marry him, and that would be the ruin of everything.

But if I did tell, Hog Waller would kill Blackie.

I knew that—now that Dony had pointed it out. He'd killed other men for less.

I tried to figure a way out for Blackie, but I couldn't. There didn't seem to be but one answer.

"Promise?" Dony urged.

I nodded and swallowed. "I promise," I said.

"Good boy!" Dony said. "And you won't let Spud tell?"

"I won't let Spud tell," I said.

Dony bent and put her warm lips against my face. "I love you, too, Cotton!" she whispered. "When I have my first boy, I'm going to name him after you!"

At daylight, Dave Wilson was asleep in the fire-place room, and I left Spud gnawing on a biscuit and searching the house over for his lost cap. I went outside where the menfolks were feeding and hooking up teams, getting ready to go into town for the wedding.

The wind had died and big feathery snowflakes were falling thick and fast. The ground was too warm yet and most of the flakes melted as soon as they hit, but on the fence posts and roofs and on the dry cow chips scattered about they were beginning to stick and pile up, making everything look white and strange.

I went out to where Blackie and Dony were sorting mine and Spud's stuff out of the buckboard into Papa's big wagon. Papa had given them the loan of the dun mare and buckboard till they got married and settled.

Doc Cole had patched up Blackie's head before he'd passed out under the kitchen table. The white bandage covered nearly all of Blackie's head except the ducktail and made him look like a snow-capped fence post walking around. He worked silent, with a puzzled frown creasing the skin between his eyebrows. Now and then, when he thought Dony wasn't looking, he shot her a wondering glance. Like maybe he couldn't get her figured out.

Dony finally caught him at it and her mouth began to tremble. Her face got all torn up and she started laughing and crying at the same time. She caught him by one arm and looked up at him.

"I wanted you bad, Blackie," she said. "But I never would have done this to you. It was just that I didn't see how else to keep you from getting shot!" She hushed her laughing and crying and kept looking up at him, trying to make him believe her.

Blackie stood holding a bedroll on one shoulder, looking down at her and then away. "Why, it ain't nothing to bother about," he said. "The slickest kind of an old fox'll keep fooling around a bait till he finally gits caught. I got by longer'n most!"

"But I wanted you to want me!" Dony said.

Blackie shifted the bedroll to his other shoulder. "Why, now, as to that," he said. "I been wanting you bad enough all along. It's just that a man sure hates to give in and take on a big load of responsibility."

His eyebrows drew together in a worried frown. "You take right now," he said. "I'm bothered about not having no sleeping mattress. It don't hardly look right, bringing a woman home to nothing but a bunch of old ragged bed quilts piled on a hard floor!"

He reached down to finger the hole in the knee of his pants, but he still had on his party clothes and there wasn't any hole there, so he reached up and pulled his ducktail instead.

"Now, of course," he went on, "Brother Joe's got a patch of scrap cotton we could pick us a sleeping mattress out of, soon as this weather breaks. But it'll sure be a sight of work!"

"Not for me, it won't," Dony said eagerly. Then she bragged: "It won't take me no time to pick and make us a mattress. I'm a fast cotton picker. I'm fast with a needle and thread, too!"

243

Blackie's face cleared and he smiled. "Well, now," he said brightly, "if you can fix us up with a sleeping mattress, we'll make out fine. We sure will!"

Mama and Papa came out and stood with me at the front-yard gate to watch the wedding party get off to town.

Blackie and Dony went first, sitting close together in the buckboard seat, wrapped up in a quilt. Back of them trotted Rock and Drum, heads down, tails high in the air. Then followed Fiddling Tom and his woman, with Mexico Jesus and his panther-claw scar I never did get a close look at. Then came the Dooleys and the Fikeses, the Newtons—Doc Cole, riding off in his buggy, red faced and shaky, but happy over a bottle of whisky somebody had dug up for him.

Hog Waller and his woman—they'd pulled out right after the fight.

Mama wanted us to stay. Mama said somebody had to help out Rachael at a time like this. Dave had to be taken care of. There was house cleaning to be done, clothes to wash.

So we stood and watched till the falling snow hid the last wagon and then listened to the rattle of the wheels over the rocky road.

It's all over, I thought miserably. *Blackie's gone. If it'd been a fighting bull, Blackie could have stood his hack. If it'd been a bunch of old bad hogs or a scrapping river coon—anything in the woods— Blackie could have handled it. But it was people. And Blackie wasn't cut out to handle people.*

I knew it would never be the same now. Blackie wouldn't get to prowl when and where he wanted to any more. There'd always be a woman with him— or waiting for him to come in. There'd never be another coon hunt like this that had started out so fine. Me and Spud—we'd never get to go live with Blackie in his shack on Birdsong Creek. We'd never get to learn all the big secrets of the woods.

My throat was dry and aching. I couldn't seem to get my breath. The black pup, full as a tick on fresh meat, came trotting around the corner of the house. He came up and licked my hand and sat down beside me, facing down the canyon road. He listened to the rumble of the wagon wheels and started whining, finally to howling a little.

The tears started coming, and I couldn't stop them.

Papa looked down at me and must have understood some of what was on my mind. He put a hand on my shoulder and gripped it tight.

"A man can't romp and prowl all his life," he said soberly. "It ain't natural, son. Comes a growing-up time, when it's nothing but right for him to step between the traces and pull his part of the load."

Mama said: "Cotton's a mighty little boy to have a hard lesson like that stuffed down him, Aaron."

"He'll have it to learn," Papa said. "Sooner or later!"

"Then it can be later," Mama said shortly. "He's still just a boy. Our only boy, Aaron!"

Papa pulled one horn of his mustache into his mouth and chewed on it, staring at Mama out of the corners of his eyes. "Yeah?"

I stared at Mama, too. What was she fussing at Papa about?

Mama's face got red. She whipped off her bonnet and started twisting the strings around her hands.

"Well, I mean he's got plenty of playing time left before he grows up," she said. "We can give him things he wants and he can play with them and not have to worry for a long time yet!"

"Yeah?" Papa said again. "What sort of things, Cora?"

Mama's eyes blazed. "You know what I'm getting at, Aaron Kinney!" she flared. "I don't see why you keep pestering. I mean Cotton's our only boy, and if he's eating his heart out for that old black hound-pup, then he can have it!"

She wheeled and hurried toward the house, calling back over her shoulder, "But I'm warning you both right now! You better never let me catch him scratching up my flower beds!"

Papa said sternly: "You hear that, boy? You ever let that old black pup scratch up a flower bed and your mama'll have us doing some tall stirring around!"

He winked at me, then followed Mama back into the house, grinning.

Nigger reached up and licked my hands. I went down beside him, holding him tight. And under my hand I could feel his heart thumping fast and strong, matching the beat of my own!